THE ILLUSTRATED WORLD OF TOLKIEN

THE SECOND AGE

To my uncle and aunt, Marvyn and Judy Day

Thunder Bay Press
An imprint of Printers Row Publishing Group
9717 Pacific Heights Blvd, San Diego, CA 92121
www.thunderbaybooks.com • mail@thunderbaybooks.com

Text copyright © David Day 2023
Artwork, design and layout copyright © Octopus Publishing Group Ltd 2023

Printers Row Publishing Group is a division of Readerlink Distribution Services, LLC. Thunder Bay Press is a registered trademark of Readerlink Distribution Services, LLC.

Correspondence regarding the content of this book should be sent to Thunder Bay Press, Editorial Department, at the above address. Author and illustration inquiries should be addressed to Pyramid, an imprint of Octopus Publishing Group Ltd, Carmelite House, 50 Victoria Embankment, London EC4Y 0DZ
www.octopusbooks.co.uk

THUNDER BAY PRESS
Publisher: Peter Norton
Associate Publisher: Ana Parker
Editor: Dan Mansfield

PYRAMID
Publisher: Lucy Pessell
Senior Editor: Hannah Coughlin
Contributing Editor: Robert Tuesley Anderson
Assistant Editor: Samina Rahman
Designer: Isobel Platt
Senior Production Manager: Peter Hunt

Illustrations by Victor Ambrus, Jaroslav Bradac, Rachel Chilton, Tim Clarey, Alan Curless, John Davis, David Frankland, Melvyn Grant, Barbara Lofthouse, Pauline Martin, Mauro Mazzara, Ian Miller, Andrew Mockett, Turner Mohan, Andrea Piparo, Peter Price, Kip Rasmussen, David Roberts, Šárka Škorpíková, Jamie Whyte, Robert Zigo

Library of Congress Cataloging-in-Publication

Names: Day, David, 1947- author.
Title: The illustrated world of Tolkien : the second age / David Day.
Other titles: Second age
Description: San Diego, California : Thunder Bay Press, [2023] | Summary:
 "An illustrated guide to the least-known period in Middle-earth's
 history, the Second Age. The lore and legends of this period are given
 life through hundreds of illustrations from artists who have studied
 Tolkien's work, and insightful commentary from David Day makes this a
 valuable addition to the shelf of anyone with a keen interest in
 exploring more of Tolkien's world"-- Provided by publisher.
Identifiers: LCCN 2022054618 | ISBN 9781667203379 (hardcover)
Subjects: LCSH: Tolkien, J. R. R. (John Ronald Reuel),
 1892-1973--Encyclopedias. | Middle Earth (Imaginary
 place)--Encyclopedias. | LCGFT: Encyclopedias.
Classification: LCC PR6039.O32 Z4595 2023 | DDC 823/.912--dc23/eng/20230206
LC record available at https://lccn.loc.gov/2022054618

ISBN: 978-1-6672-0337-9

Printed in China
27 26 25 24 23   1 2 3 4 5

THE ILLUSTRATED WORLD OF TOLKIEN

THE SECOND AGE

DAVID DAY

THUNDER BAY
P·R·E·S·S
San Diego, California

PART TWO

PART THREE

INTRODUCTION

No reader of *The Lord of the Rings* (1954–5) can fail to notice how the past grows ever more present in its unfolding story. Beginning in the idyllic Shire, landscapes increasingly bear witness to the events of thousands of years before that have continued to resonate down through the centuries: from the desolate Weathertop – the site of an ancient Númenórean fortress – where Frodo and his companions are attacked by the Black Riders, to the ruins of the once-powerful Elvish kingdom Hollin, in the western shadows of the Misty Mountains, to the Dead Marshes that seemingly preserve the bodies of Elves slain during a great and terrifying battle, Middle-earth wears it history close to its surface. Individuals, too, have their origins in the ancient past – Elrond, now Rivendell's arch-sage and counsellor, was long ago a warrior and herald in ancient wars, and Aragorn is the descendant of a long line of now-dispossessed kings whose dynasty can be traced back six thousand years and more. And there are the artefacts: great swords like Narsil, the scrying stones known as the Palantíri, and, above all, the Rings of Power, including the Three Elven Rings and the One – all tying the fate of the present to a destiny laid down in Middle-earth's deepest history.

The origins of these places, people and artefacts lie in a 3,500-year period of Middle-earth history known as the Second Age. Over three decades and more, from the 1930s on, Tolkien carefully constructed a body of "history" that not only enriches our reading of his fictions depicting the (late) Third Age but which also stands in its own right as a great and distinctive narrative. Of all Middle-earth's ages, however, the Second Age is perhaps the least known: while the posthumously edited and published *Silmarillion* (1977) is dominated by mythological tales of the First Age and *The Hobbit* (1937) and *The Lord of the Rings* give an account, in novel form, of the culminating years of the Third, there is no all-encompassing fiction for the Second Age. We have, principally, the chronology of the age given in Appendix B of *The Lord of the Rings*; the 30-page *Akallabêth* that comprises the fourth part of *The Silmarillion*, and the narrative fragments and lists of people in and events of the Second Age published in *Unfinished Tales* (1980), as well as the extensive notes published in *The History of Middle-earth*, principally volume five, *The Lost Road and Other Writings* (1987), which includes the earliest version of the Downfall of Númenor. Apart from the *Akallabêth*, these are fragmentary and, to a degree, unresolved, and for this reason the Second Age has long remained something of a "dark age" for Tolkien's readers: lost between the mythology of the First and the epic fiction of the Third, its full grandeur was only slowly revealed to the public through the painstaking, almost archaeological efforts of Tolkien's son and literary executor, Christopher.

The Second Age is made up of two great narrative channels: on the one hand the rise and cataclysmic downfall of the island-kingdom of Númenor and its aftermath, and on the other the forging of the Rings of Power and the rise to power of the new dark lord, Sauron. The first – essentially Tolkien's powerful reimagining of Plato's story of Atlantis – had haunted the writer for much of his creative life and provided the one sustained, complete narrative of the Second Age, the *Akallabêth*. The second – in some ways more crucial as providing the deep background of *The Lord of the Rings* but nonetheless rather more hazily recorded – relates the story of the Elf Celebrimbor's forging of the Rings of Power and Sauron's attempt to co-opt the rings' power by forging his own, the One, in the fires of Orodruin (Mount Doom). Both channels eventually run together to provide the climax of the Second Age: the War of the Last Alliance (3429–3441 SA) between, on one side, the Elves and so-called Faithful among the

Númenóreans (miraculous survivors of the cataclysm) and, on the other, the forces of Sauron – Southrons, Easterlings and Black Númenóreans among them. Tolkien has not quite left us a narrative account of the war, but its outlines and principal turning points – the bitter Battle of Dagorlad and the fatal double duel between Elendil and Gil-galad and Sauron on the slopes of Mount Doom – have a mythic power and imaginative resonance that make us wish that Tolkien had actually written a complete poetic "Fall of Gil-galad", whose beginning is recalled by Sam in *The Lord of the Rings*.

Tolkien's sources for his Second Age are, of course, as rich and varied as ever. Beyond the avowed influence of the myth of Atlantis, the author drew deeply not only from his vast knowledge of European history, mythologies and languages, but also from his own personal experience: the seed of his Downfall of Númenor, for example, was his recurring dream of a green island overwhelmed by a great wave, while the gruelling Battle of Dagorlad is informed by his participation in the Battle of the Somme. We find, too, the writer's lifelong concern with the philosophical, theological and societal problems of evil and power as well as with the destructiveness and allure of war. Tolkien, "high fantasist" though he is labelled, was no escapist, and his Second Age bears the scars of grief and loss as much as, say, the mournful *The Children of Húrin* (2007) or the more elegiac passages of *The Lord of the Rings*.

Our task in the following book, then, is to uncover and delve into some of these influences and show how the power of Tolkien's imagination is manifest even in the lesser-known parts of his legendarium. The work of the excellent artists and illustrators who have contributed so much to this book, brilliant and evocative as it is, is also testament to just how fiercely Tolkien's genius continues to burn.

WARRIOR
IAN MILLER

PART ONE

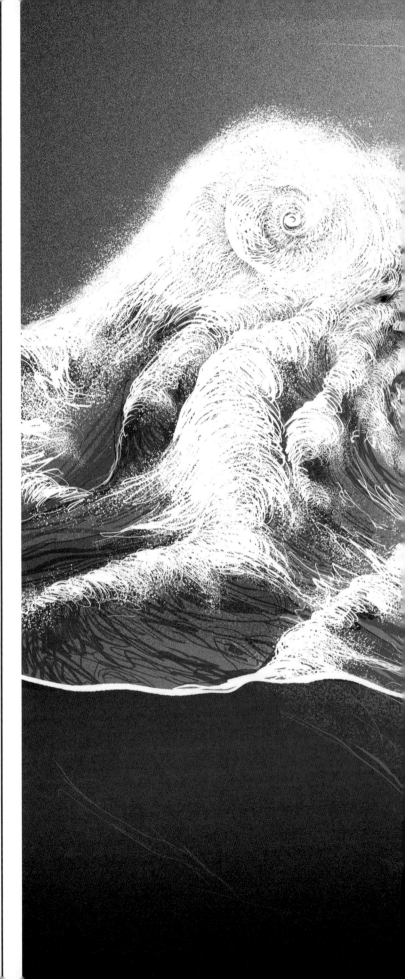

A CHRONOLOGY OF THE SECOND AGE

1 Foundation of Lindon, under Gil-galad

32 Foundation of Númenor, with Elros as its first king

c. 500 Sauron reappears in Middle-earth

c. 750 Establishment of Eregion (Hollin) by Celebrimbor

c. 775 Foundation of Vinyalondë, the first Númenórean haven in Middle-earth

1000 Sauron begins to build Barad-dûr, the Dark Tower, in Mordor

c. 1350 Galadriel and Celeborn settle in Lothlórien

1590 Celebrimbor forges the Three Rings

1600 Sauron forges the One Ring – the Year of Dread

1693 The War of the Elves and Sauron begins

1697 Fall of Eregion and the foundation of Imladris (Rivendell)

1700 Númenóreans defeat Sauron at the Battle of Gwathló

1701 First White Council is held

2709 Ar-Adûnakhôr is the first Númenórean king to take an Adûnaic royal name

3117 Númenóreans ban the use of the Elven tongue

3177 Civil war breaks out in Númenor between the King's Men and the Faithful

3255 Ar-Pharazôn seizes the Sceptre

3262 Ar-Pharazôn takes Sauron prisoner

3319 Downfall of Númenor and the Changing of the World;
Sauron flees back to Middle-earth

3320 Foundation of the Realms in Exile, Arnor and Gondor

3430 Last Alliance formed between the Númenóreans in exile and the Elves

3431 Last Alliance marches to Imladris

3434 Battle of Dagorlad followed by the Siege of Barad-dûr

3441 Deaths of Gil-galad and Elendil; defeat of Sauron; Isildur takes the One Ring

NÚMENÓREAN VOYAGE
DAVID FRANKLAND

THE FOUNDING OF NÚMENOR

While it was the downfall of Númenor that haunted Tolkien and led to his most sustained piece of Second Age-set fiction – *Akallabêth: The Downfall of Númenor* – he also sketched out the geography and history of his island-kingdom in some detail. In this, he follows his most important and freely avowed source for *Akallabêth*, Plato's story of the island of Atlantis, found in his dialogues *Timaeus* (c. 360 BCE) and the fragmentary *Critias*, in which the Greek philosopher describes, through his titular mouthpiece, not only the drowning of an ancient island kingdom but also charts its geography and constitutional setup.

By imagining a 3,000-plus-year backstory for Númenor, Tolkien is able not only to provide further potency and pathos to his moralized history of an ideal state corrupted by human greed and pride but also a magnificent, poignant background that echoes down through subsequent millennia in the history of Middle-earth. Even the sheltered Hobbits of the Shire – if Merry, Pippin and Sam are anything to go by – seem to be dimly aware of the splendour and tragedy of "Westernesse" and its tall, grim Men with their bright swords.

The principal source for the foundation of Númenor is *Unfinished Tales* (1980), edited by Christopher Tolkien, although there is important information, too, in both *The Silmarillion* and Appendix A of *The Lord of the Rings* as well as in other posthumously published notes and materials.

NÚMENOR AND THE SECOND AGE IN PRINT

So far as the general public was concerned – and readers of *The Hobbit* in particular – Númenor only came into existence in 1954 with the publication of the first volume of *The Lord of the Rings* – and then, only as a kind of rumour of an ancient unknown age. For despite having been conceived and named nearly two decades before in Tolkien's "The Lost Road" (not published until 1987 as *The Lost Road and Other Writings*), Númenor first appears in print in *The Fellowship of the Ring*, when readers hear of the legendary existence of the ancient lost realm in Gandalf's revelation of the history of the One Ring.

In the second volume, *The Two Towers*, as the adventurers wander among the ruined citadels and monuments that were rumoured to be raised by those ancestral kings, we come to understand a little more of the bloodline linking Gondor to the Númenóreans. While in the final volume, *The Return of the King*, there are more allusions to Númenor, and we discover that Tolkien has passed on his dream of the great wave to Faramir the Steward of Gondor. And ultimately, we at last come to fully appreciate how significant Strider/Aragorn's Númenórean genealogy is in his claim to the crown – and indeed, in justification for the title of the third volume: *The Return of the King*.

Nonetheless, in the actual narrative of this epic tale, readers of *The Lord of the Rings* have no idea of how fully conceived Tolkien's history of the Númenóreans and their descendants was until they discover the quite astonishing Appendices A and B at the back of the third volume. In sixty pages of densely compressed type, Tolkien's "Annals of the Kings and Rulers" and "The Tale of Years" presents the histories and chronologies of the kings of Númenor and their descendants and allies over the 6,000-year span of the Second and Third Ages.

And in fact, that cataclysmic event marked by the Great Wave – so essential to a full appreciation of Tolkien's legendarium – did not appear in its final form as the *Akallabêth: The Downfall of Númenor* for another 22 years, when it was finally published posthumously in *The Silmarillion* in 1977. Then too, further accounts and histories of Númenor only appeared (edited by his son Christopher) over the next two decades. In 1980, *Unfinished Tales of Númenor and Middle-earth* gave readers their first map and geographic description of Númenor, as well as the tale of "The Mariner's Wife" and biographical notes on all of Númenor's rulers. In 1987 in *The Lost Road and Other Writings* – the earliest drafts of *The Fall of Númenor* and the opening chapters of the abandoned *Lost Road* appeared.

In 1992, in *Sauron Defeated*, readers were provided with the full text of "The Notion Club Papers" and a variation on Númenor's downfall called "The Drowning of Anadûnê". And then, in 1996, *The Peoples of Middle-earth* was published as the twelfth volume in The History of Middle-earth series. Then, quite unexpectedly, after a hiatus of 25 years, yet another volume of Tolkien's fragmentary notes and drafts related to the history of Arda appeared in 2021 and a further book on Númenor, *The Fall of Númenor*, was published in November 2022.

c. 1900
Tolkien experiences his first "Atlantis-haunting" dream

1936–7
Tolkien begins *The Lost Road*, a time-travel work in which he first conceives of Númenor

1945–6
Tolkien revisits the themes of *The Lost Road* in a new novel, *The Notion Club Papers*

1951–5
Tolkien drafts and redrafts *The Tale of Years*, a chronicle of the major events of the Second Age

THE EARLY GENESIS
OF NÚMENOR AND
NÚMENOR AND THE
SECOND AGE IN PRINT

1954 *The Lord of the Rings* I. The Fellowship of the Ring	1955 *The Lord of the Rings* III. The Return of the King	1977 *The Silmarillion*
1980 *Unfinished Tales of Númenor and Middle-earth*	1984 *The Book of Lost Tales*	1987 *The Lost Road and Other Writings*
1992 *Sauron Defeated*	1996 *Peoples of Middle-earth*	2021 *The Nature of Middle-earth*

THE EARLY YEARS OF NÚMENOR

32 The first Edain of Beleriand reach Númenor

32 Elros becomes king as Tar-Minyatur, first king of Númenor

442 Death of Elros Tar-Minyatur

c. 500 Sauron returns to Middle-earth

600 Vëantur makes the first voyage back to Middle-earth, to the haven of Mithlond

725 Aldarion makes his first journey to Mithlond in a ship captained by Vëantur

750 Aldarion founds the Guild of Venturers

c. 775 The foundation of Vinyalondë, the first Númenórean haven in Middle-earth

870 Aldarion and Erendis are married

882 Aldarion and Erendis separate

883 Tar-Aldarion becomes king

1000 Sauron begins to build Barad-dûr, the Dark Tower, in Mordor

1075 Queen Tar-Ancalimë becomes the first ruling queen

A PROMISED LAND

The Númenóreans were the survivors of the Three Houses of the Edain – the Men who fought alongside the Elves in the Wars of Beleriand at the end of the First Age. After the destruction of Beleriand, the Valar – Tolkien's deity-like Powers – offer the Edain recompense and haven in the form of a new homeland, on a great island created for them far out in the Western Sea. A promised new homeland cannot but invite a comparison with the Promised Land of the Tanakh (Hebrew Bible), first promised to Abraham in Genesis and then to Moses in Exodus, as he leads the Israelites out of slavery in Egypt to Canaan, the "Land of Milk and Honey". Númenor likewise is the Land of Gift – Andor, the Elves' name for the island.

The Númenóreans reach their new home in ships piloted by Elves, following the Star of Eärendil, known to the Edain as Rothinzil, the equivalent of our Evening and Morning Star (the planet Venus). The real-world planet-star has ancient religious significance, worshipped as a goddess or god, including Ishtar in ancient Babylonia. Later, the Morning Star – Phosphorus, the bringer of light – was associated with Christ, a sign of hope and resurrection in the dawn sky – associations of which Tolkien, a committed Catholic, would have been sensible to. The following of a star to a holy place also reminds us of the Three Kings or Magi following the Star to Bethlehem, to pay homage to the Messiah.

All of these connotations emphasize the fact that the creation and colonization of Númenor signals the hope of a new age. However, they are not without a dark underbelly. The ancient Romans also called the Morning Star Lucifer – like Phosphorus, meaning the "Light-bringer" – which in Christianity was the name given to Satan before his fall from Heaven. Likewise, Númenor, for all its promise of a bright future for Man, will eventually fall due to the machinations of Tolkien's Satan, Sauron.

FROM "STARWARDS" TO "DOWNFALLEN"

Somewhat uncharacteristically, the Elves give the new island a quite literal name – Andor, Land of Gift. The Edain, for once, are more poetic. Because of the means by which they first came to their new island home, they first called it Elenna, meaning "Starwards" in Quenya (*elen* is the root word for star, though with a secondary meaning of Elf). To underline the starry connections of his island, Tolkien also gave his island the shape of a five-pointed star; the original name of its first king, too, is Elros, meaning "star-foam". The island's association with guiding stars may remind us of the Star of Bethlehem, which leads the Magi to the Messiah – Jesus Christ – who will usher in a new age on Earth. Númenor, too, enacts the promise of a new age.

Later, the new inhabitants do give Elenna an altogether more prosaic name, Númenórë/Númenor, in Quenya, or Anadûnê, in Adûnaic (the language of the Númenóreans) – all meaning "West-land". This became Westernesse, in Tolkien's "translation" of the name into English. After its destruction, the Elves called the island Atalantë – a name that playfully, if rather directly, associates the island with the very similar-sounding Atlantis.

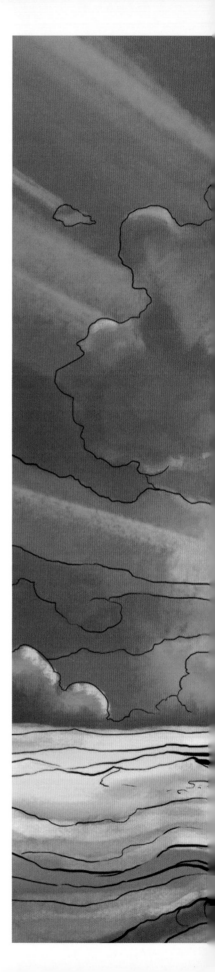

STARWARDS
MAURO MAZZARA

LAND OF THE STAR — NAMES AND PENTACLES

In *The Return of the King* (1955), the third volume of *The Lord of the Rings*, readers discovered extensive appendices that included the Annals of the Kings. Here, Tolkien explained how the Edain – the noble and heroic Men who survived the wars of the First Age – sailed westward over the Great Sea and "guided by the Star of Eärendil" came at last to "the great Isle of Elenna, western most of all Mortal lands". And it was on that great island continent that the Edain settled and founded the kingdom of Númenor.

However, it was not until the posthumous publication of *The Silmarillion* (1977) – some forty years after Númenor's original conception – that readers learned the name Elenna could be translated from Elvish to mean "starwards", or "Land of the Star". This revelation left readers with the impression that the island was so called because of the guiding light of the "Star of Eärendil". And yet, this was far from being the full story.

Readers would have to wait another four years for the publication of the second posthumous book, *Unfinished Tales of Númenor and Middle-earth* (1980), to learn the most obvious explanation for the name Elenna "Land of the Star" was, in fact, geographic. In *Unfinished Tales*, it is explained for the first time: "The land of Númenor resembled in outline a five pointed star, or pentacle."

And indeed, Númenor's geography was roughly mapped out in the form of a pentacle or pentagram: a five-pointed star enclosing a pentagon – a five-sided regular polygon that has five equal sides and five equal angles. The pentagram contains ten points: five points of the star, and five points of the vertices of the inner pentagon. Drawing diagonal lines between the points of a pentagon results in a perfect star shape most often known as a pentagram, but also a pentacle, pentalpha and star-pentagon.

This account – also for the first time – is accompanied by a map of the star-shaped island along with an extensive description of the geographic, horticultural, political and social organization of Númenor. Readers are also informed that the central portion measured "some two hundred and fifty miles across, north and south, and east and west, from which extended five large peninsular promontories." Based on these measurements, one might roughly calculate the area of this star-pentagon shaped island. And if one wished to make a real world comparison, this would suggest Númenor had a landmass equal to twice the size of the main island of Great Britain.

The map published in *Unfinished Tales* was created by Christopher Tolkien many years after his father's death. That map was based upon the father's written texts and an unpublished "little rapid sketch, the only one, as it appears, that my father ever made of Númenor". Consequently, the published map, although not entirely authoritative, provides an adequate model for Númenor's overall geography along with the location of its major cities, harbours and provinces. There are detailed aspects of the map: its shore-line, for instance – as acknowledged in its unmapped haven of Almaida along with its unmapped system of roads – that must be left open to speculation.

The star pentagram was a symbol deeply rooted in antiquity. Certainly, it was a symbol celebrated in the earliest civilizations in Mesopotamia, Babylon and the Indus Valley. Most famously, the five-pointed star pentagram was the symbol and sign of recognition for the Brotherhood of the Pythagoreans. Pythagoras was the sixth-century BC Greek philosopher and mathematician whose thinking had a profound influence on the thinking of Socrates, Plato and Aristotle. To the Pythagoreans the star pentagram revealed the mathematical-mystical secret of the ideal world of the golden ratio, perfect proportions and ideal forms.

Each of Númenor's provinces were largely determined by their alignment with the geometric divisions of a pentagram. Númenor's central region was roughly the shape of the central five-sided pentagon. This was known as Mittalmar or "Inlands" and was the kingdom's royal capital. Each of the five peninsular promontories (each roughly shaped isosceles triangles) were princely realms known as: Forostar or "Northlands", Andustar or "Westlands", Orrostar or "Eastlands", Hyarnustar or "Southwestlands", and Hyarrostar or "Southeastlands".

When *Unfinished Tales* finally revealed the geometric shape of Númenor to his readers, it is worth noting Tolkien's description of the island as "a five-pointed star, or pentacle". It is interesting that he chose the rather arcane word "pentacle" to describe the island, rather than the more common "pentagram". This has considerable significance related to Tolkien expertise in Medieval Christian iconography. In 1925, Tolkien and the Canadian philologist E V Gordon published the Oxford Press scholarly edition of the fourteenth-century Middle English poem *Sir Gawain and the Green Knight*: a work that Tolkien would later fully translate in verse. In that poem, we have the only description in Medieval literature of the pentacle inscribed upon the shield of Gawain. And as Tolkien would have noted: this was the first instance of the word "pentacle" being employed in the English language. Furthermore, according to the poem's narrator, the pentacle was the sacred symbol inscribed on the Seal of King Solomon. As such, each of its five points represented the five virtues of knighthood that Gawain exemplified: generosity, friendship, courtesy, chastity and piety. It also related to the five senses and five fingers, the five wounds of Christ, and the five joys of Mary and Joseph experienced in the birth of Christ.

As Tolkien was obviously aware, the pentacle was also adapted by witches and sorcerers for evil purposes by rotating the symbol so the two points of the star projected upward. Its reversal was emblematic of the triumph of matter over spirit: the goat of lust attacking heaven with two horns. It was important to keep the five-pointed star upright with its topmost triangle pointed to heaven. Considering the history of Númenor, its rise to power as an ideal utopian state and its ultimate corruption and downfall, the star pentagram seems to be predetermined by its geometry and geography. In occult circles the pentagram within a circle was a trap for demons, but as revealed in Christopher Marlowe's *Doctor Faustus*, an imperfectly drawn pentagram will allow the demon to escape. As Númenor's pentagram is only roughly drawn in its geography, perhaps this may have been a factor in the fate of Númenor's King Ar-Pharazôn whose captive Sauron – like Faustus's demon Mephistopheles – seduces and ultimately destroys his master.

ANDÚNIË
PETER PRICE

ISLANDS OUT OF THE SEA

In Plato, Poseidon, the Greek god of the sea, created Atlantis, or at least fashioned its major features, including its city, and was its guardian deity. This is mirrored in Tolkien's Númenor, where it is the Maiar Ossë – a spirit of the sea – who causes the island to rise out of the sea, though we may well wonder why it is not Ossë's lord, the Valar Ulmo, King of the Seas, who does not perform this task. Both spirits admittedly have a long history of helping the Children of Ilúvatar.

Elsewhere in Greek mythology, Poseidon also creates the island of Delos, at the request of Zeus, as a resting place for the pregnant Leto, the mother-to-be of Artemis and Apollo. The divine creation of islands is found in many other real-world mythologies, too. In the ancient Japanese text known as the Kojiki, a male–female pair of gods, Izanagi and Izanami, create the first piece of land, Onogoro-shima, after stirring the sea with a heavenly spear: when they lift the spear out of the sea, a few drops fall back into the sea creating the island on which they subsequently marry. The Polynesians likewise told many cosmological myths of god-created islands.

In *Timaeus* and *Critias* Plato gives a detailed account of the geography of Atlantis, although the details are somewhat confusing and contradictory. It lies, he tells us, in the Atlantic Ocean (*Crit*. III 109.a), in front of the Pillars of Hercules (*Tim*. III 24.e) – the term given in antiquity to the promontories on either side of the Strait of Gibraltar – and is larger than Libya (meaning North Africa) and Asia (meaning Asia Minor) combined. It is part of an extensive archipelago, over which it rules and for which it serves as the capital. Atlantis also ruled Europe up to Thyrrenia (usually identified as Etruria in Italy) and Libya from the Pillars to the border of Egypt (*Tim*. III 25.b). Atlantis is dominated by a vast plain, three thousand stadia (some 345 miles or 550 km) long and two thousand stadia (230 miles or 370 km) wide. To the north of the island is a chain of mountains while the south is split by a long channel that ends in the open sea (*Crit*. X 118.b).

Elements of Plato's Atlantean geography can be recognized in Tolkien's Númenor, as described in the chapter "A Description of Númenor" in *Unfinished Tales*, where Tolkien is clearly emulating both Plato's description, though in far more poetic vein. Tolkien's island – properly called Andor, Land of Gift – lies, like Atlantis, in a western sea, Belegaer ("Great Sea") – but takes the distinctive form of a five-pointed star, five massive promontories that stretch out into the sea. Like Atlantis, again, it is dominated by a central plain, at the centre of which is the Holy Mountain, Meneltarma (Pillar of Heaven), overlooking the capital, Armenelos.

Once again, like Atlantis, the north of the island is mountainous and the south split by a body of water: in Númenor, the River Siril that flows south from Meneltarma to a delta land of reedy marshes and meres. In this last detail, we may be reminded of the geography of ancient Egypt, with the River Nile and its delta.

Tolkien gives a detailed description of his island's regions, each of which has its own distinctive character. Thus, the somewhat bleak, forested, mountainous Forostar – Northlands – is contrasted, for example, with the near-treeless grasslands of Mittalmar (Inlands), the most populous region, and with the balmy fertile wooded areas of Andustar, around the Bay of Eldanna.

ARMENELOS

Before the foundation of the Númenórean kingdom and its capital, Armenelos, the Edain had built no cities, nor had lived in them as a community. In Beleriand, they had lived in small settlements and farmsteads. The first Mannish city, Armenelos, then, must have been built on Elvish models, such as Gondolin or Eglarest, and almost certainly using Elvish skills and knowhow. We might perhaps imagine it to be "Egyptian" in appearance, built in a massive, monumental style, as Tolkien describes in his letter to Rhona Beare, though it was probably without fortifications, as there was no real external threat, at least in its earliest stages. It was titled "the Golden", perhaps owing to the colour of its stone rather than because of any golden decoration. There are two known buildings, the Great House of the Kings and their associated courts (home of the White Tree, Nimloth), and Númenor's final days, the great domed Temple dedicated to the worship of Morgoth.

Armenelos must have in turn served as the model for the many imperial Númenórean cities built during the Second and Third Age, from Annúminas, the capital of Arnor, to Osgiliath, capital of Gondor – forming a mighty network of military and political powerhouse across the west of Middle-earth.

ANNÚMINAS
PETER PRICE

MENELTARMA
PETER PRICE

MENELTARMA: THE HOLY MOUNTAIN

Tolkien may have taken some of his inspiration for his geography of Númenor from a seventeeth-century map of Atlantis, created by the Jesuit scholar Athanasius Kircher (1602–80) and published in Amsterdam in 1669. It is very basic and bears little resemblance to Plato's description of the island – its most salient feature, apart from a few rivers, is a tall mountain at the centre of the island. This may be behind Tolkien's siting of Meneltarma, the Pillar of Heaven, at the heart of Númenor.

Meneltarma overlooks the capital, Armenelos, and was the holiest place on the island, reserved for the worship of Eru Ilúvatar, the creator god in Tolkien's legendarium. Such holy mountains abound in civilizations across the world – from Mount Zion that overlooked the ancient walls of Jerusalem, to Mount Ararat in present-day Armenia, where Noah's Ark was said to have come to rest, to Mount Fuji in Japan and Uluru in Australia. As holy places, such places were stepped on lightly and in great reverence, and Tolkien's Meneltarma, too, was visited only without tools or weapons – only the king was allowed to speak there. Its summit was guarded by eagles – called the witnesses of Manwë – just as Mount Olympus was guarded by Zeus's eagles.

The peak of Meneltarma was said to be the only part of Númenor to survive the final cataclysm – as an islet in the Belegaer. This may be a reminiscence of Mount Ararat, which from medieval times was thought to be the resting place of Noah's Ark when the rest of the world had been flooded.

THE NATURAL WORLD OF NÚMENOR

Tolkien was a keen botanist and created a rich flora as a backdrop for his tales, in part based on real-world species and in part on invented ones. Thus, while Plato gives us only a brief account of the natural world of Atlantis – emphasizing only the abundance of "fragrant things there are in the earth, whether roots, or herbage, or woods, or distilling drops of flowers or fruits, grew and thrived in that land" – Tolkien gives us an almost lyrical account of his island's various biomes, mapping them carefully onto its geography.

Each of Númenor's regions has its own biome. Forostar is a mountainous land of firs and larch and heathered moors; Mittalmar a near-treeless expanse of grasslands and pastures; Hyarrostar a territory of woods and wide white beaches; the warm south-easterly Hyarnustar has a Mediterranean-type landscape of vineyards, and in the cool north-easterly Orrostar was the primary source of the kingdom's grains. The most lavishly described region, however, is Andustar, especially the balmy, rainy area around the Bay of Eldanna named Nísimaldar. Here the wealth of species of trees and plants – many of them introduced from Tol Eressëa, the island home of many of the Eldar, near Valinor – is at once so diverse and intense that we might think of the Cape floral kingdom at the southern tip of South Africa – Tolkien's native country – with its more than 9,000 plant species.

OLVAR:
FLORA OF ARDA

Flowers

Elanor

Lissuin

Niphredil

Alfirin

Mallos

Simbelmynë

Plants

Seregon

Galenas

Athelas

Trees

Culumalda

Brethil
(Birch)

Gallows-
weed

Lauriniquë

Vardarianna

Brambles of
Mordor

Neldoreth
(Beech)

Mallorn

Oiolairë

Yavannamirë

Region
(Holly)

Nessamelda

Lairelossë

Trees of
Valar

Tasarion
(Willow)

Taniquelassë

A BOTANICAL TREASURE-TROVE

Tolkien loved nature. As a child he learned botany from his mother and liked nothing better than to ramble through the countryside about his Midlands home, getting to know its plants and flowers. He transposed this love into his writing: when reading *The Lord of the Rings*, as we follow the progress of his characters through the vast and varied landscapes of Middle-earth we, too, become immersed in its natural world. We feel the rich earth underfoot in the Shire, we become entangled in the brambles and nettles of the Old Forest, and we gaze across to the haze of the Misty Mountains on the far horizon. We experience every kind of weather, too – from the unsparing rains that seep through the seams of the travellers' clothes, to the knuckle-blistering blizzards on Mount Caradhras, to the scorching sunshine of southern lands like Gondor.

The reader's imaginative immersion in nature is made possible by Tolkien's meticulous and deeply empathic descriptions of the living landscapes of his continent and the trees, plants and herbs that flourish there. Nature, in *The Lord of the Rings* especially, is as much a character as the Hobbits, Men and Elves who live and depend on it. There is plenty of luminous detail – from the smooth silver-grey bark of the mallorn trees of Lothlórien; to the long, pungent leaves of athelas, or Kingsfoil, used to treat Frodo's Morgul knife wound; to the brakes of old brown fern that Frodo and Sam bed down in the shadows of the mountains of Mordor. Nature feels inhabited – literally so in the case of the Ents, Tolkien's walking trees.

Mostly based on the real-world species of northern Europe, the botany of Middle-earth is enriched with species more or less invented, sometimes supernatural – many, like the mallorn and athelas, introduced from Aman or Númenor. Tolkien was also careful to vary his flora from region to region, land to land, so that, for example, each of his forests or woodlands are distinctive from the others. Lothlórien and Fangorn are only a few dozen miles from each other but are entirely different as biomes: the former spacious and bright and full of flowers (the white-flowered niphredil and the golden star-shaped elanor) and the latter dim, musty, cramped – like the Old Took's study, as Pippin comments.

FRAGRANT LANDS, FRAGILE WORLDS

Tolkien describes the trees and plants of Nísimaldar in lyrical detail. Many of the blossoming trees have Elvish names derived from the queens of the Valar – *vardarianna* (named for Varda), *yavannamírë* (for Yavanna) and *nessamelda* (for Nessa). In what is perhaps a nod to Plato's own fragrant island, throughout his description Tolkien emphasizes the fragrance the trees and flowers create – the name Nísimaldar, indeed, means "Fragrant Trees".

Perhaps the most famous tree that grows in Nísimaldar – well known, that is, to readers of Tolkien's *The Lord of the Rings*, is the gigantic, silver-trunked *malinornë*, whose leaves are silver in summer but gold in autumn and winter, never falling until the tree blossoms gold in spring. It is this tree that will astound the Ring-bearer and his Hobbit companions when they arrive in Lothlórien thousands of years after the Downfall of Númenor, in the Third Age. Seeds of the mallorn, Tolkien tell us, are passed from the sixth king, Tar-Aldarion, to his friend Gil-galad, High King of the Elves of Middle-earth, and from him to Galadriel, who will eventually plant them in her forest realm.

This careful treasuring and passing on of seeds is Tolkien's way of impressing on us the fragility of the natural world, in need of careful nurturing if it is to survive the ravages of industrialization and other human activity. All Tolkien's works, written years before the modern environmentalist movement, are imbued with an ecological consciousness. The Downfall of Númenor, he seems to say, is not only a human catastrophe, but an environmental one too: many of the species he describes flourishing in Númenor will be forever lost to Middle-earth. Only through Tar-Aldarion's happenstance gift is something of the beauty of Númenor saved for Middle-earth – at least for a time. With the passing of Galadriel over the sea the mallorns of Lothlórien will also eventually dim and die.

ELVES AMONGST THE MALLORNS
VICTOR AMBRUS

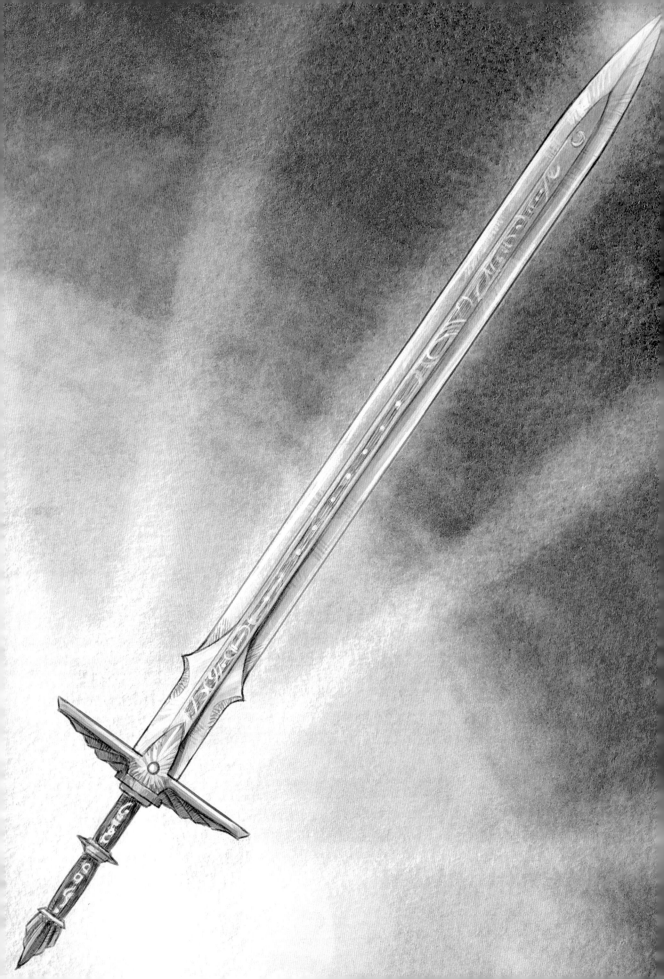

NARSIL
MAURO MAZZARA

METALLURGY

In his "Description of Númenor", Tolkien spends some time talking about metal and metallurgy – again, it seems, in parallel to a similar passage in Plato's *Critias*. Atlantis is rich not only in gold and silver but also in orichalcum, which in Greek means "mountain copper", a rather mysterious metal that is mentioned several times in ancient literature but which was, Plato tells us, no longer mined in his time. It is sometimes described as white – and so might be platinum – but sometimes as yellow, too – hence some argue the name was meant to designate brass or a copper alloy.

Tolkien, by contrast, goes out of his way to tell us that Númenor largely lacked mineral wealth. Early in their history the Númenóreans knew of gold and silver and jewels only from the gifts of the Elves. The island does have deposits of iron and copper, and Númenórean smiths, taught by the Noldorin Elves, learned to make weapons, such as the sword given to the King's Heir. (Tolkien here seems to be making a buried reference to Narsil, the Númenórean longsword of King Isildur, whose broken shards will be reforged for Aragorn as Andúril towards the end of the Third Age.)

Orichalcum gets no mention in accounts of Númenor but may well have influenced Tolkien's conception of mithril – the silvery, immensely hard, yet lightweight, hyper-precious metal mined by the Dwarves in Khazad-dûm.

EGYPTOMANIA

Tolkien thought of the peoples of his legendarium as to some degree reflecting historical civilizations and cultures: the Rohirrim, for example, have strong similarities with the Anglo-Saxons; the Gondorians of the Third Age have an undeniable Greek or Roman bent; and the barbarian peoples of the east of Middle-earth (such as the Wainriders) have a kinship with the invading Goths and Mongols.

For the Númenóreans, Tolkien took his inspiration primarily from the ancient Egyptians, as he revealed in a letter to the classics scholar Rhona Beare (1935–2018). The Númenóreans, he told Beare, were "proud, peculiar and archaic"; they had a passion for the monumental and the massive and had the technology to back this up; they were interested "in ancestry and in tombs", and he explicitly compares the tall, winged Númenórean crown to the pschent, the distinctive double crown of Egypt, which was likewise worn at an angle. While Tolkien was writing here specifically of the "Númenóreans of Gondor", it is hard not to deduce that Númenórean civilization, in its entirety and from its very beginnings on its island home, had the self-same flavour.

The Egyptian influence on Tolkien's conception of the Númenóreans might be traced back to the story of Atlantis itself. In Plato's dialogue *Timaeus*, the Athenian statesman Solon is told the tale of the lost island and civilization by an old priest in the Egyptian city of Sais. The Atlanteans, from their base out in the Atlantic Ocean, had built up a mighty empire on the European mainland, subjugating its peoples, including, for a time, the ancient Egyptians, and leaving their mark on their culture. The ancient Egyptians certainly seem to have thought of their own civilization as deriving from another powerful, still more ancient people than themselves.

The Egyptian flavour of Tolkien's Númenóreans may also reflect the renewed wave of Egyptomania that swept Europe in the wake of Howard Carter's discovery of the tomb of Tutankhamun in 1922 (there had been an earlier craze for all things Egyptian after Napoleon's campaign in Egypt in 1798–1801). During the 1920s "Tutmania", as it was dubbed, gripped Europe and the United States, inspiring everything from ancient Egypt–set films and novels to jewellery and clothes featuring Egyptian motifs. President Hoover even named his Belgian Malinois dog King Tut in honour of the boy-pharoah. Tolkien, too, with his passion for ancient civilizations, was probably not entirely immune from this "mania" and allowed it to colour his emerging conception of Númenor from the late 1930s.

Once we know this Egyptian connection, we begin to see echoes of it everywhere in Tolkien's account: in the monumental architecture of the capital, Armenelos, in particular the 500-foot-high Temple (not a gold-capped pyramid, admittedly, but golden-domed, yet similarly spectacular and associated with a death cult; in the long list of dynastic rulers with their grandiose-sounding names, the pharaoh-like Ar-Pharazôn, the last king of Númenor among them; in the Valley of the Tombs, Noirinan, where the Númenórean kings and queens were buried; and in the highly centralized, king-oriented culture, and in the sporadic queens who were able to rule in their own right. The Holy Mountain at the centre of Númenor, Meneltarma, is pyramid-like in shape and proportions, and may have been inspired by the ziggurats of Mesopotamia, artificial holy mountains built to connect heaven and earth, humanity and the gods, themselves possible models for the Egyptian pyramids.

THE NÚMENÓREANS AND THE HEBREWS

Egypt was by no means the sole inspiration for the Númenóreans. In his letter to Rhona Beare mentioned previously, Tolkien points out that, while the Númenóreans should be pictured as Egyptian, in theology they were "Hebraic" – by which he means, we can infer, that they worshipped not a plethora of deities but a single god. For almost all of the history of Númenor, this god was Eru Ilúvatar – the supreme creator; only in the final days did the Númenóreans turn to Melkor, "Lord of All, Giver of Freedom", the evil spirit cast out from Arda at the end of the First Age. Eru, like Yahweh, was associated with and worshipped on a mountain. In the Bible, the Hebraic god, Yahweh, speaks to Moses on Mount Sinai and mountains were his sacred spaces, like outdoor temples – "The mountain of the Lord's house", (Micah 4:1). Likewise in Númenor, Eru is reverenced in a vast hallow on top of Meneltarma, "The Pillar of Heaven", where none but the king could speak. The Hallow of Eru, Tolkien tells us, is completely unadorned – without temple or altar or even a raised pile of stones, a description that may recall the biblical commandment against graven images.

There are other elements drawn from the biblical Hebrews, too – Tolkien wrote that the non-Elven language of Númenor, Adûnaic, was based on Hebrew; the kings of Númenor, especially in their longevity, recall the patriarchs of Genesis (of whom there is a similar number – 20 against the 25 Númenórean kings), and parallels can be drawn between Israel as the home of the Chosen People and Númenor as the Land of Gift. The downfall of the proud Númenóreans, after their idolatrous worship of Morgoth, has its parallel in the Babylonian Exile of the Israelites, punished for idolatry and disobedience to the one god, Yahweh.

ISLANDS: UTOPIAS AND DYSTOPIAS

Islands have been an important draw for the human imagination since earliest times – they have appeared in works of philosophy (Plato's island-kingdom of Atlantis in the dialogues *Timaeus* and *Critias*), in novels (Daniel Defoe's *Robinson Crusoe* or Robert Louis Stevenson's *Treasure Island*), in plays (William Shakespeare's *The Tempest*) and, of course, in countless myths and legends, from Avalon, last resting place of King Arthur, to the Islands of the Blessed in Greek mythology.

The island is by its very nature – removed from the mainland and out in an ocean or a lake – mysterious and alluring. No child can resist the thought of living on an island, as the Swallows and Amazons of Arthur Ransome's eponymous novel prove. Islands are often paradises – "The isle is full of noises," says *The Tempest*'s wild man Caliban, "Sounds, and sweet airs, that give delight, and hurt not" – and they are sometimes the settings for ideal communities, or utopias, as described, for example, in Sir Thomas More's *Utopia* (1516), about an imaginary ideal island-state in the New World. They can also, however, be hells and dystopias. In the mysteries of an island sometimes peril lurks, as in H. G. Wells's *The Island of Doctor Moreau* (1896) where the island is home to a mad scientist who creates animal–human hybrids, or the island in William Golding's *The Lord of the Flies* (1954), where a group of stranded schoolboys descend swiftly into violence and savagery.

While the primary island-model for Tolkien's Númenor is Plato's Atlantis, many other island elements seem to have influenced his depiction of it. Númenor begins as a kind of paradise or utopia – an Isle of the Blessed summoned out of the waves as a reward for the deeds of the Houses of Men during the Wars of Beleriand. The island is of unparalleled beauty, its people live long and untroubled lives, and it is ruled by wise and virtuous kings. Only over many centuries does the island civilization take a darker turn, as the kings and many of their subjects grow too powerful and covetous. Tolkien's island story is, to a degree, an allegory for the unavoidable fall of humankind – from a state of grace to cataclysm brought about by human folly.

From Tolkien's description of Númenor, in its primary state, before its corruption, it is clear that he intended it as a kind of ideal utopian state. The word "utopia" was coined by the English humanist and philosopher Sir Thomas More in his fiction-cum-satire *Utopia* (1516) and means "No Place", but with a secondary pun on the Greek for "good place" (*eutopia*). More's and Tolkien's island share, admittedly, very few features – it is hard to imagine the Númenóreans tolerating multiple religions or running a welfare state, as do the Utopians – but both authors are concerned to show what a good commonwealth might look like – "a place of felicitie", as More writes, or "the bliss of Númenor", as Tolkien writes. And for many hundreds of years, Númenor is just such a place. However, as both More and Tolkien might have agreed, "no place" such as this could really endure. Númenor is doomed from the start.

ELROS AND ELROND
MAURO MAZZARA

STARRY-EYED TWINS

Tolkien conceived of Elrond – later to be the Elven ruler of Rivendell – and Elros – the first king of Númenor – as twins. As children of Half-elven parents, Eärendil and Elwing, they were given the choice of choosing either the fate of the Elves – immortality – or the fate of Men – the gift of death.

Tolkien's semi-divine twins take clear inspiration from mythological forebears, perhaps most clearly Romulus and Remus, who likewise have alliteratively paired names. In Roman legend, Romulus and Remus were the sons of the god Mars and Rhea Silvia, a princess of Latium, who were famously suckled by a she-wolf and went on to found the city of Rome. Elros and Elrond likewise stand at the beginning of the civilizations of the Second Age – Elros as the forefather of the Númenórean kings and Elrond as one of the forefathers of the remnants of the High Elves in Middle-earth.

Except in their choice of fates, there is no sense of conflict between the brothers as there is between Romulus and Remus. It is the latter who, after a dispute with his brother, is killed either by his brother, Cain and Abel–style, or by one of his supporters.

The choice of Elrond and Elros can be associated with another pair of mythological twins, Castor and Polydeukes (Pollux), the sons of Leda: Castor, as the son of Tyndareus, king of Sparta, was mortal, while Polydeukes, as the son of Zeus, was immortal. Like Elrond and Elros, too, they have starry connections: Elrond's name means "star-dome" in Sindarin, and Elros, "star-foam", while Castor and Polydeukes were eventually transformed into the constellation Gemini.

Unlike the fully fleshed-out Elrond, whose star is allowed to shine in *The Hobbit* and *The Lord of the Rings*, Elros remains a somewhat shadowy figure, as perhaps befits the forefather of an ancient dynasty (rather like the obscure first Egyptian pharaoh, Narmer). On becoming the first ruler of Númenor at the age of ninety, he assumes the Quenya name Tar-Minyatur – high-first ruler – and rules for 410 years, making him the longest-lived Man in the legendarium (if we discount the unnaturally extended lives of the bearers of the Nine Rings, the Nazgûl). The first king of Plato's Atlantis, incidentally, was named Atlas, the son of Poseidon and the mortal Cleito.

While Elros is undoubtedly a Man of the Second Age, his twin brother, Elrond, really comes into his own only in the Third, where, as we know, he plays an important role in both *The Hobbit* and *The Lord of the Rings*. (Elves have much longer to grow up, so the trajectories of the brothers' lives are enormously different.) That is not to say that Elrond does not play a key role in Tolkien's chronology of the Second Age. Indeed, he appears as a much active, heroic figure at this stage, before his later incarnation as an éminence grise of the High Elves: as the captain and herald of Gil-galad in Lindon, as the leader of the Elvish army that seeks to aid Eregion (but arrives too late to do so), as the founder of Rivendell as a High Elven refuge, and, of course, again as Gil-galad's herald in the Last Alliance.

Soon after the foundation of Rivendell, Gil-galad entrusts Elrond with Vilya, the Ring of Air, the most powerful of the Three Rings – perhaps betokening the future importance of Elrond and his haven-realm of Rivendell as custodian of the High Elven tradition.

TAR-MENELDUR
ŠÁRKA ŠKORPÍKOVÁ

LIFESPAN OF THE NÚMENÓREANS

In *Unfinished Tales*, Tolkien tells us that the Númenóreans were granted a lifespan three times that of ordinary mortals. Using the biblical allotment of human life "three score years and ten" (Psalm 90) as our measure, this would make the Númenórean lifespan 210; female Númenóreans lived slightly longer still. The ruling family – the descendants, through Elros, of both Men and Elves and even of a Maia, Melian – lived even longer, around twice that of their subjects. Elros, who admittedly spent his youth as a Half-Elf, lived until he was 500 and then only voluntarily gave up his life.

The longevity of the Númenórean kings in particular cannot fail to remind us – especially when we consider the Hebraic elements that Tolkien gave their culture – of the biblical patriarchs of Genesis, who lived spectacularly long lives. God created Adam and Eve as immortal – just as the Númenórean Elros might have been if he had chosen a different path – but they became subject to death after their expulsion from Eden. Still, Adam lived for 930 years, Noah for 950, and Methuselah – whose name has become a byword for venerable age – 969. After Noah and the biblical Great Flood – a story that influenced Tolkien's account of Númenor – the lifespan of the patriarchs diminished rapidly. Noah's son, Shem, the eleventh patriarch, lived until he was "only" 600 and Abraham, the twentieth patriarch, until he was "just" 175.

Over the years, the lifespan of the kings dwindled – while Elros's son Vardamir Nólimon lived until 410, the twenty-fourth king, the Elf-loving Tar-Palantir, lived for only 220. Númenórean blood gave longevity into the Third Age and beyond. The Chieftains of the Dunedain lived for some 150 years (if they did not die by violence). Aragorn, the sixty-fourth descendant of Elros, lived for the classic Númenórean number of years – 210. With Aragorn, then, there is a restoration to something of the blessed existence of Númenóreans at the beginning of the Second Age.

LISTS OF KINGS

Unlike the thirty dynasties of pharaonic Egypt, Númenor has just one – lasting from 32 SA to 3319 – just under 3,300 years. Pharaonic Egypt, likewise, lasted for some 3,000 years, though with far less continuity of rule. In Appendix A of *The Lord of the Rings* Tolkien published, in the context of a brief overview of Númenórean history, a list of its kings and queens, as part of the "Annals of the Kings and Rulers". The list is given again, with some discrepancies, as "The Line of Elros", in the posthumously published *Unfinished Tales*, though here each reign is given its own summary.

Such lists, or annals, of rulers have been made since the most ancient times, a fact of which Tolkien was well aware and seems to be emulating here (as if his list is itself a found record). To mention but a few, there was an ancient Sumerian List of Kings; the Saqqara Tablet lists fifty-eight rulers of Egypt from Anedjib and Qa'a (First Dynasty) to Ramesses II (Nineteenth Dynasty), while the Old Testament has plenty of annal-type elements, including lists of the kings of Israel and Judah. In Ireland, the eleventh- or twelfth-century text *Lebor Gabála Érenn (The Book of Invasions)* lists the high kings of Ireland, including many purely mythological ones.

KINGS AND QUEENS OF NÚMENOR

1. Elros Tar-Minyatur
532–422 FA
32–422

2. Tar-Vardamir
61–471
422

3. Tar-Amandil
192–603
422–590

4. Tar-Elendil
350–751
590–740

5. Tar-Meneldur
543–942
740–883

6. Tar-Aldarion
700–1098
883–1075

7. Tar-Ancalimë
873–1285
1075–1280

8. Tar-Anárion
1003–1404
1280–1394

9. Tar-Súrion
1174–1574
1394–1556

10. Tar-Telperiën
1320–1731
1556–1731

11. Tar-Minastir
1474–1873
1731–1869

12. Tar-Ciryatan
1634–2035
1869–2029

13. Tar-Atanamir
1800–2221
2029–2221

14. Tar-Ancalimon
1986–2386
2221–2386

Tar-Abducal (Herucalmo)
2286–2657
2637–2657
Considered a usurper and therefore not counted as one of the kings

15. Tar-Telemmaitë
2136–2526
2386–2526

16. Tar-Vanimeldë
2277–2637
2526–2637

17. Tar-Alcarin
2406–2737
2637–2737

18. Tar–Calmacil/Ar-Belzagar
2516–2825
2737–2825

19. Tar-Adramin/Ar-Abattârik
2618–2899
2825–2899

20. Ar-Adûnakhôr
2709–2962
2899–2962

21. Ar-Zimrathôn
2798–3033
2962–3022

22. Ar-Sakalthôr
2876–3102
3033–3102

23. Ar-Gimilzôr
2960–3177
3102–3177

24. Tar-Palantir
3035–3255
3177–3255

25. Ar-Pharazôn
3318–3319
3255–3319

TAR-MINASTIR
PETER PRICE

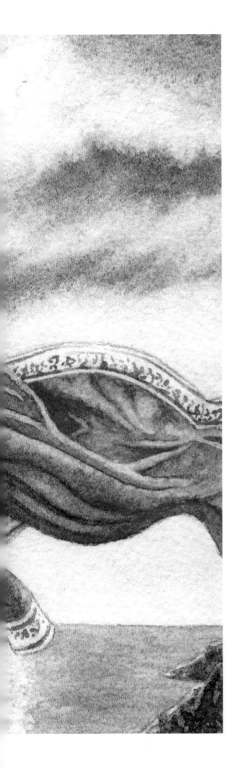

THE NATURE OF KINGSHIP AND THE HOUSE OF ANDÚNIË

Typically, rulers acquire their position after the death of their predecessor and retain rule until their deaths, unless deposed – this, at least, has been the case among European monarchs, at least until the late twentieth century (setting aside the abdication of the British king Edward VIII). In his ideal island, Tolkien seems committed to a different model of kingship in which freedom and autonomy combined with self-renunciation are crucial to the nature of the ideal ruler. Following the path laid down by the first king, Elros, the kings traditionally surrendered the Sceptre to their heir some years before their death, before the decay of old age had set in, and likewise surrendered their lives before death took them by force, so to speak (Tolkien may have taken this idea from Thomas More's *Utopia*, where euthanasia is practised). Númenor's long fall from grace begins, it seems, when Tar-Ciryatan forces his father to pass on the kingship and is compounded when his son, Tar-Atanamir, refuses to relinquish both the Sceptre and his life and dies enfeebled while still king. At this point, Númenórean kingship decays from a life of service into a lust for power and self-aggrandisement – to reach its nadir in the reign of the maniacal Ar-Pharazôn, the last king.

Throughout the history of Númenor, the Lords of Andúnië exist as a shadow, distaff dynasty to the main royal line, highlighting, through their loyalty and piety, how far the kings were drifting away from the kingdom's foundational ideals. They traced their descent to Silmariën, eldest daughter of the fourth king, Tar-Elendil, who married Elatan, lord of the port-city of Andúnië in the west of the island. Such junior lines have been common in European history and could act as a powerful rival power base to the throne, even on occasion succeeding to it. One of the best-known examples is the House of Bourbon, which was descended from a younger son of the Capetian king of France Louis IX (reigned 1226–70), but which came to power itself with the accession of Henry IV in 1589. The Lords of Andúnië, while the second-most powerful family in the land, were, however, unswervingly loyal to their king – until the increasingly impious and hostile rule of the later kings made it impossible for them to remain so, leading to their becoming the secret leaders of the Faithful. Nonetheless, in the final Lord of Andúnië, Elendil, and his sons, this junior branch did finally come to power, albeit in the Númenórean Realms-in-Exile, thereby preserving all that was most noble about the Men of Westernesse.

NÚMENÓREAN LANGUAGE

One of Tolkien's scholarly day jobs was as philologist. Not content with the grammar schoolboy's ancient Greek and Latin, as a student and beyond he studied and mastered an enormous variety of languages, including many dead ones – among others, Old Norse, Anglo-Saxon, and Gothic – together with living languages such as Finnish and Welsh. He was fascinated, too, by how languages developed and connected with one another.

Unsurprisingly, then, he created a similar linguistic richness for his own imaginary world, sometimes using elements from real-world languages as his inspiration. Thus the sound-structure, or phonology, of his Elvish language Sindarin was based on Welsh, while, in its music, Quenya has a clear relationship with Finnish, even if its vocabulary is completely different. For Tolkien, these two Elven languages, in particular, became like living languages, diverse and evolving, and capable of deep poetic expression.

While the elite of Númenor spoke the Elvish languages – at least during the first almost 3,000 years of its history – and had Quenyan names, the island also had its own language, Adûnaic, or properly Adûnayân: the "Language of the West". This derived from some of the languages spoken by the Men of Beleriand, which were collectively known as Taliska. While Tolkien did not expend as much energy and effort on developing Adûnaic's vocabulary and grammar as he did his Elvish languages, he nonetheless gave it a pronounced flavour, which he described as being based on Hebrew.

Tolkien would not have needed to look far to see how language, which is so entwined with cultural and ethnic identity, could become a political matter. In the late nineteenth and early twentieth century, nationalist movements across Europe sought to revive languages and cultures that had been buried or suppressed by more powerful neighbours. In Ireland – then a colony of Britain – there was the Gaelic revival that went hand in hand with the move towards independence; in Catalonia, the Renaixença movement, which sought to revive Catalonian language and culture in the face of Castilian Spanish hegemony; and in Finland, an ongoing "language strife" between Swedish – the language of the ruling classes – and Finnish, the language of the peasants, which only ended in 1923, when Finnish finally acquired an official status equal to Swedish in the new republic.

In Númenor, likewise, language becomes a bitter bone of contention, as there is an upswell of a kind of Númenórean nationalism against the Elvish culture and the power of Valar. The twentieth king of Númenor adopts an Adûnaic name – Ar-Adûnakhôr – and forbids the use or teaching of Elven-tongues. Only the so-called Faithful continue to use the Elven languages in secret. Almost all later kings used the prefix Ar- rather than the Quenya Tar-, meaning much the same thing: "high" or "king". Of course, the linguistic nationalism of the late Númenóreans runs counter to our usual sympathies – Adûnaic is associated with the blasphemous, prideful rebellion against the Valar and far less with an assertion of cultural identity in the face of colonial or hegemonic powers.

A descendant of Adûnaic, Westron, is the lingua franca of Middle-earth, spoken by Men, Hobbits and Elves (in non-Elvish company) through the Third Age and beyond. It thus holds the place of English in our world – the language, of course, that Tolkien used to translate it.

ENGLISH / ADÛNAIC glossary wheel:

- wizard — zigûr
- orc, goblin — uruk
- beloved — zìrân
- sun — ûri
- the West — adûni
- shadow — ugru
- death — agan
- dog — raba
- king or queen — Ar-
- gold — pharaz
- king — ârû
- elf (lit. "shining one?") — nimir
- power/goddess — avalê
- soldier — nardû
- power/god — avalô
- conqueror — kathu-phazgân
- to wage war — azgarâ-
- horse — karab
- sea — azra
- woman — kali
- sea-lands — azra-zâin
- city — kadar
- ship — balak
- Earth — daira
- star — gimli

53

ELVEN KING WITH HIS DAUGHTERS
VICTOR AMBRUS

PRIMOGENITURE

In its earliest days, Tolkien tells us, the kingship of Númenor was governed by the principle of agnatic (male) primogeniture – succession by the eldest son or nearest male relative – apparently in imitation of the High Kings of the Noldorin Elves (we may think of the Salic laws of the medieval Franks, which explicitly forbade inheritance by women). This rule was overturned by Tar-Aldarion – the first king not to have a son – who introduces absolute primogeniture, succession by the oldest child whatever their sex. This is a rule of succession unknown to real-world monarchies – until 1980, when Sweden amended its Act of Succession, followed, over the intervening decades, by most of the other European dynasties. Tolkien's Númenor seems almost revolutionary in this respect. The practice may reflect the strong Platonic influence on Tolkien's kingdom: in the Greek philosopher's *Republic* he suggests that women, while physically weaker than men, can be trained to be guardians of the state just as well as men.

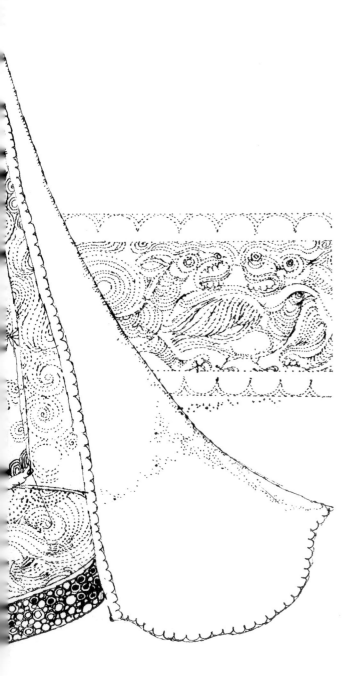

RULING WOMEN

Tolkien's world, as has often been observed, is overwhelmingly patriarchal, and the many dynasties he listed – whether the kings and stewards of Gondor, the High Kings of the Elves, the royal houses of the Dwarves, or the Thains of the Shire – are entirely male. The one exception is the royal dynasty of the Númenóreans where three Ruling Queens are listed among the twenty-five rulers in the "Line of Elros" – four if we include Tar-Míriel, who by right ought to have succeeded to the Sceptre. The exception may well be due to the Egyptian caste Tolkien gave to his island-kingdom: four female pharaohs from the native dynasties of Egypt – Sobekneferu (c. 1807–1802 BCE), Hatshepsut (c. 1479–1458 BCE), Neferneferuaten (c. 1334–1332 BCE) and Twosret (c. 1191–1190 BCE) – are known to have ruled in their own name, though there may have been others lost to history, while many more acted as regents.

Despite the somewhat revolutionary aspects of succession, Tolkien, who, we may note, was born during the reign of one queen (Victoria) and died during the reign of another (Elizabeth II), often describes the Ruling Queens in terms that we might think of as sexist. Thus, the first Ruling Queen, Tar-Ancalimë (reigned 1075–1280), is described in "The Line of Elros" as "proud and wilful" – qualities that, after all, might be considered normal in a male king. She neglects the good policies of her father, Aldarion, not continuing his friendship with Gil-galad and the Noldorin Elves on the mainland, for example. She is likewise shown as unnatural enough to resist marriage for a very long time. The next Ruling Queen, Tar-Telperiën (reigned 1556–1731), seems to be noteworthy only for her Elizabeth I–like resistance to marriage altogether. (By some curious coincidence, Elizabeth I began her reign in 1558 in our era, just two years after Tar-Telperiën.)

The remaining Ruling Queens belong to the later, darker years of Númenor and fare in Tolkien's eyes little better than their predecessors. Tar-Vanimeldë neglects her role as queen, giving her time to enjoy music and dance – a neglect that leads her husband, Herucalmo, to seize the throne after her death, thereby deepening the crisis in the kingdom. Tar-Míriel, who is loyal to the old ways of Númenor, has a much darker fate: her cousin Ar-Pharazôn seizes the Sceptre and marries her against her will.

Through the figure of Tar-Míriel – daughter of the reformist twenty-fourth king of Númenor, Tar-Palantir, and unwilling wife of Ar-Pharazôn, the twenty-fifth – Tolkien prevents his narrative of the Downfall of Númenor from seeming too black and white, with only the evil punished and the good saved, as in a medieval morality play. In the final cataclysm, Tar-Míriel – the rightful ruler of Númenor under the Law of Succession – climbs the Holy Mountain, Meneltarma, but is cruelly swept away by the great wave. The scene seems ambiguous – does she climb the mountain merely to save herself or to draw closer to Eru the One? Is she punished because she has failed to stand up to her husband and protect the Faithful – a party to which she belonged? Or is she merely innocent collateral in the wrath of Eru against the Númenórean people? If the latter, then her death seems to raise long-standing philosophical/theological issues about the nature of an omnipotent deity – why does he not always save the good, and how can he let evil happen? Whatever Tolkien's intention, Tar-Míriel's death provides a memorable, moving image in the unfolding tale.

We may feel that her pathetic death as she attempts to climb Meneltarma to avoid the Great Wave that bears down over Númenor is an unwarranted punishment meted out on a victimized woman by a vengeful male god. Númenor, as Tolkien has his heroine Erendis complain in the tale that bears her name, is a place fashioned by men.

CÍRDAN THE SHIPWRIGHT
VICTOR AMBRUS

ANCIENT SEAFARERS

Plato's Atlanteans were great seafarers, hopping between the islands of their archipelago and establishing a mighty empire that stretched deep into the Mediterranean Sea. Tolkien's Númenóreans, by contrast, took some time to establish their seafaring credentials, perhaps surprisingly given Elros's pedigree as the son of Eärendil the Mariner. However, the Edain more generally, Tolkien makes clear, were not natural seafarers and were first brought to the island, he tells us, in boats piloted by Elves under the command of Círdan the Shipwright. It took some 700 years before the first Númenórean ships returned to Middle-earth, pioneered by Vëantur, Captain of the King's Ships under Tar-Elendil, the fourth king. Tar-Elendil's grandson, Tar-Aldarion, was the Henry VIII of Númenor; like the English king he was the Great Shipbuilder. From that time on, Númenor was to become a powerful seafaring nation, in a position to explore Middle-earth and set up colonies, much as the English navy would be the foundation of the later British Empire.

Perhaps the most pertinent real-world comparison for Númenórean sea power, however, is the Phoenicians – a people of the first millennium BCE whose homelands were in what is now Lebanon but whose prowess as mariners and traders led them to set up colonies hundreds of miles away in the western Mediterranean – in Sicily, Sardinia, North Africa and southern Spain, including the famous city of Carthage. There is a long tradition, dating to ancient times, of identifying the Atlanteans as an offshoot of the Phoenician people.

ALDARION AND ERENDIS

In his published writings, Tolkien was most often clearly drawn to the world of the epic, especially in its medieval incarnations – long, martial poems such as the Anglo-Saxon *Beowulf*, the Middle High German *Nibelungenlied* or the Icelandic sagas. The dragon-slaying Bard the Bowman in *The Hobbit* seems to be inspired by the faithful Wiglaf in *Beowulf*, while the ambitious Boromir in *The Lord of the Rings* is a tragic character who would not be out of place among the doomed families of the *Nibelungenlied*.

However, Tolkien also took inspiration from other medieval genres, most notably the Arthurian romance – the tale of adventure and courtly love that reached its most perfect expression, perhaps, in the writings of the twelfth century French poet Chrétien de Troyes. We can see some of these courtly elements in Tolkien's work, in the love stories of Beren and Lúthien in *The Silmarillion* and, especially, the Arwen–Aragorn–Éowyn love triangle in *The Lord of the Rings*. We find it, too, in the unfinished Númenórean tale of "Aldarion and Erendis", a paired title that is reminiscent of both Chrétien de Troyes's *Érec et Énide* (1170) and a slightly earlier Welsh tale, *Culhwch ac Olwen*.

Apart from the tale of Númenor's downfall, *Akallabêth*, included as the fourth part of *The Silmarillion*, "Aldarion and Erendis" is the only sustained, substantial tale from the "matter of Númenor", as we might call it. Even then, as presented in *Unfinished Tales*, it breaks off towards its end, only "completed" by Christopher Tolkien in the form of extended notes. Unlike the other Tolkienian romances – which typically show the nobility and stoicism of lovers in the face of adversity – "Aldarion and Erendis" has a bitter note, especially in its depiction of its frustrated heroine, Erendis, "The Mariner's Wife" of the subtitle.

In many ways the story takes up the basic trope of the Arthurian romance, where the hero is caught between the private duties of love and the public duties of knighthood. Aldarion, the heir to the throne of Númenor, is shown constantly deserting his lover (and later wife), Erendis, to set sail and explore the coastlands of Middle-earth, forging friendships with the Elves, in particular Gil-galad, while leaving Erendis increasingly lonely and embittered. In the Arthurian romance the tensions are usually resolved and the lovers live happily ever after; in "Aldarion and Erendis", by contrast, the lovers finally separate and Erendis withdraws from court with their sole child, Ancalimë, even before Aldarion is crowned king.

The tale begins to hint at the rise of Sauron in Middle-earth – Aldarion is forging alliances and building bases against a possible conflict. In meta-narrative fashion, Tolkien even explains the survival of the tale into later ages because of its importance in the political history of the continent. The stage is set for the final cataclysm.

THE MARINER'S WIFE
TURNER MOHAN

THE COLONIZATION OF MIDDLE-EARTH

Tolkien was born when the British Empire was still in full swing, the son of a colonial bank manager in Bloemfontein, in the Orange Free State, then part of the Empire and now part of South Africa. The author was no stranger, then, to imperial rule, and while he no doubt supported many aspects of the Empire he was also more than capable of critiquing it as well – especially with regard to the arrogance and racism displayed by the white colonial classes to the non-white colonized people, as some of his letters show.

His ambivalence towards imperial ventures is likewise clear in his portrayal of the Númenórean "empire", which tracks a decline from an idealistic spirit of adventure, exploration and cooperation – as witnessed by the voyages of Aldarion as he seeks to forge friendship with the Elves against the rising power of Sauron – into the brutal exploitation of "lesser", indigenous Men, as occurs during the reign of Ar-Pharazôn. Tolkien seems to hint at the destructiveness and hypocrisy that appears to be endemic even at the very beginning of the Númenórean imperial project, when the forests about the Gwathló are felled to build ships, even as, in the island homeland, the felling of trees is banned.

THE JOURNEY
RACHEL CHILTON

THE MIDDLE-MEN

One of the more fraught aspects of Tolkien's depiction of the Númenóreans is their assumption and presumption of superiority over the Men of Middle-earth – a superiority with which Tolkien seems at least partially to concur. There is a clear "racial" hierarchy at work, even if "race" here does not necessarily pertain to skin colour.

Below the Númenóreans are the Men of western Middle-earth with whom the Númenóreans recognize a certain kinship. Known as Middle-Men, they share similar origins to the Númenóreans and speak related languages, but are far less noble and civilized. The term would be later applied to other Men who eventually became allies of the Dúnedain – such as the Northmen, from whom the Rohirrim of the Third Age descend.

At the bottom of the Mannish hierarchy – from the Númenórean point of view – are those who fall under Morgoth's and later Sauron's sway in the First and the Second Ages – the so-called Men of Darkness. These include not only the barbarian Men of the East (the Easterlings), the South (the Haradrim) and the Black Númenóreans, but also – rather more unfairly, we may think – those Men of western Middle-earth who resisted Númenórean rule, most notably the Dunlendings, who live in the wild, forgotten lands between Gondor and Arnor.

While Tolkien tacitly recognizes the inferiority of both the Middle-Men and the Men of Darkness, Tolkien also appears to be critical of the way in which the Númenóreans despoil the natural resources – especially the forests – of their lands. Tolkien, we could argue, has an acute sensitivity to environmental destruction but is rather less alert to the rights of his world's indigenous or "non-Western" peoples.

With the spotlight firmly on Númenor during most of the Second Age, the history of the Men of Middle-earth remains somewhat hazy. In some of his later writings, Tolkien may have begun to address this, suggesting that the situation in the East and South is rather less black and white than *The Lord of the Rings* and other writings portray. The Blue Wizards, he tells us, did not arrive in the Third Age along with the rest of the Istari (as he had originally envisaged) but in around 1600 SA, when Sauron began to show his hand openly. The ongoing task of the Blue Wizards, Tolkien tells us, was to persuade at least some of the Men of the East and South to break free from Sauron's yoke and thus weaken his power in his assault on the West. The ultimate success of the Dúnedain and the Elves at the close of both the Second and Third Ages was thus in part down to the good work of the elusive Blue Wizards.

UMBAR
PETER PRICE

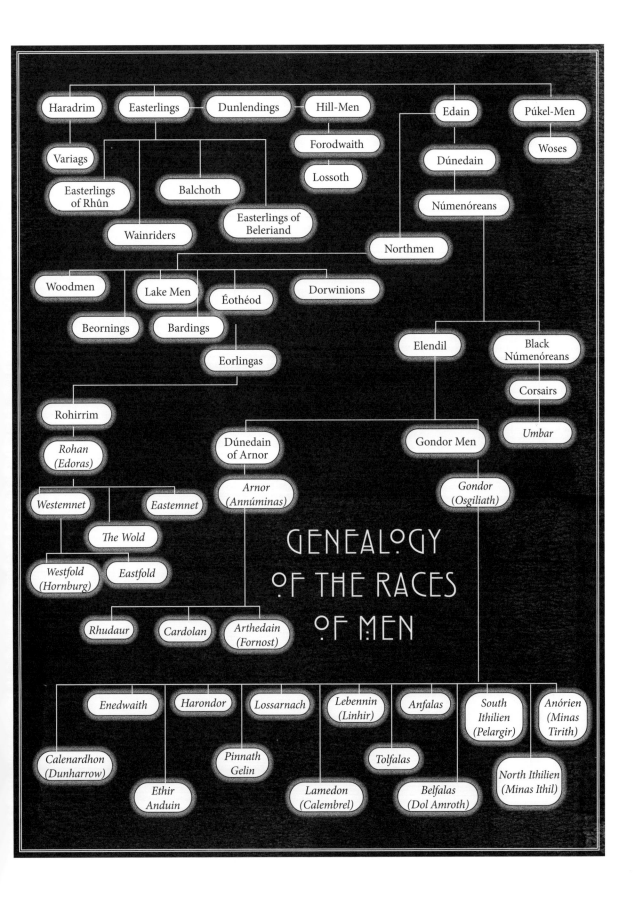

GENEALOGY
OF THE RACES
OF MEN

NÚMENÓREAN LINES OF KINGS AND LORDS

Eärendil
the Mariner

Elros
Tar-Minyatur
First King
32–442

Silmariën
*Daughter of
Tar-Elendil*

Tar-Elendil
*Fourth King,
Elf-friend of
Gil-galad*
590–740

Valandil
*First Lord
of Andúnië*
630–870

Tar-Minastir
*Eleventh King,
established the
Havens of
Umbar*
1731–1869

Amandil
*Eighteenth Lord
of Andúnië
Sailed west*
3316

Elendil
the Tall
*Nineteenth Lord
of Andúnië
Sailed east*
3319

Ar-Pharazôn
*Twenty-fifth
King*
3255–3319

3319 THE DOWNFALL OF NÚMENOR

Númenórean
realms in exile
*Elendil in Arnor, Isildur and
Anárion in Gondor*
FROM 3320

COASTAL CITIES

Through the Second Age the Númenóreans founded a number of key port-cities along the western coast of Middle-earth – first as bases from which the Númenóreans could explore deeper into the continent and later as trading posts, colonies proper, and military bases. Here we might think of the colonial city foundations in the ancient world, such as the Phoenician settlement of the western Mediterranean – at Ziz (Palermo) in Sicily or Carthage on the North Africa coast; the later Greek colonial ports in much the same area, as at Massalia (Marseilles); or the innumerable Roman port-cities founded farther afield, from Tarraco (Tarragona, Spain) to Londinium (London).

The first Númenórean settlement in Middle-earth was Vinyalondë at the mouth of the Gwathló (Greyflood), founded by Prince Aldarion towards the end of the eighth century. This was the Middle-earth base of Aldarion's Guild of Venturers – a band of Númenórean explorers and seafarers. Vinyalondë's name means "New Haven", evoking a host of real-world coastal settlements founded by European explorers in the New World from Renaissance times on, including New Haven, Connecticut, founded by English Puritans in 1638. Vinyalondë's later name, Lond Daer ("Great Haven"), by which time it had become home to vast Númenórean shipyards, echoes – coincidentally or not – London, another shipbuilding settlement in the estuary of a grey northern river, the Thames. Farther upstream from Vinyalondë was the river port Tharbad, whose main function, it seems, at least at first, was as a transportation hub for the vast swathes of timber harvested from the surrounding forests.

The port cities of Pelargir and Umbar were founded much later in the Second Age, 2350 SA and 2280 SA, respectively, and together represent almost the yin and yang, the good and bad impulses, of Númenórean culture. Pelargir – meaning Garth of Royal Ships in Sindarin – stood on the northern shore of the Mouths of the Anduin and became the base of The Faithful, those loyal to the earliest and best Númenórean traditions. Umbar, farther south, was the base of the King's Men and later the Black Númenóreans. Several real-world associations for both cities have been proposed: hot, southern, rebellious Umbar has beren frequently identified with the Phoenician city of Carthage, long a thorn in the side of the Roman Empire; and the major naval city of Pelargir, overlooking the lagoon-like mouths, with Venice, the great sea power of the medieval Mediterranean. Whether such parallels offer any illumination of Tolkien's world is another matter.

AMANDIL

Tolkien portrays several characters sailing into the West to seek mercy or aid from the Valar. Towards the end of the First Age, Eärendil sets out to find Valinor and plead for help for the Elves and Men of Middle-earth against Morgoth. This quest is repeated by Amandil, Lord of Andúnië, leader of the Faithful and Eärendil's distant descendant, in the Second: with the sacrilegious Great Armament already under way, fearing the worst for his homeland, Amandil sets sail for Valinor in a small boat to plead for the Valar's mercy.

For Tolkien, such intercessional figures may have recalled the Roman Catholic saints to whom believers pray to intercede with higher powers – God, Jesus, the Virgin – on their behalf. The characters of both Eärendil and Amandil may also have been influenced by the eighth- to tenth-century Irish epic *Navigatio Sancti Brendani Abbatis* ("Voyage of St. Brendan the Abbot") in which the titular hero sails into the Atlantic to find the "Promised Land of the Saints". Tolkien tells us that Amandil never returned, so his fate remains unknown. However, since during the Downfall his son, Elendil, and his fleet are driven towards Middle-earth by a miraculous wave, perhaps his pleas did not fall on deaf ears.

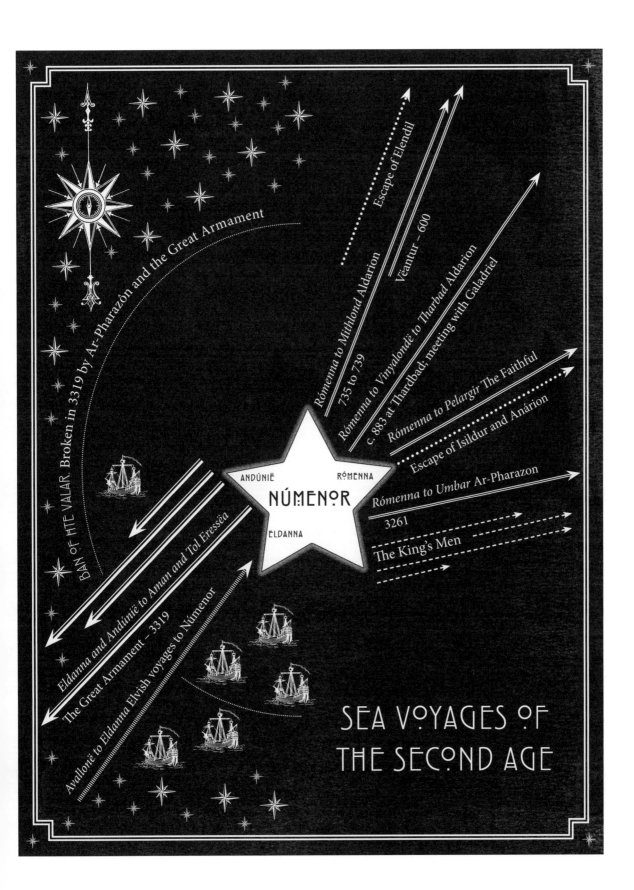

BAN ᵒF ᴛʜᴇ VALAR. Broken in 3319 by Ar-Pharazôn and the Great Armament

Escape of Elendil

Véantur – 600

Rómenna to Mithlond Aldarion
735 to 739

Rómenna to Vinyalondë to Tharbad Aldarion
c. 883 at Tharbad; meeting with Galadriel

Rómenna to Pelargir The Faithful

Escape of Isildur and Anárion

Rómenna to Umbar Ar-Pharazon
3261

The King's Men

ANDÚNIË   RÓMENNA

NÚMENOR

ELDANNA

Eldanna and Andúnië to Aman and Tol Eressëa

The Great Armament – 3319

Avallonë to Eldanna Elvish voyages to Númenor

SEA VOYAGES OF
THE SECOND AGE

PELARGIR
PETER PRICE

THE DECLINE AND FALL OF EMPIRES

That empires must eventually decline and fall is one of the rules of history, along with the idea that empires contain the seeds of their own demise, often due to the corrupting nature of great power. The archetypal empire here, of course, is Rome, whose decline was diagnosed in moral terms by early Christians on, most notably in St Augustine's City of God (426 CE). The subject of the decline and fall of the Roman Empire was taken up by Edward Gibbon in his massive history of that name (1772–89), although, even as he attacked the imperial lust for luxury, he turned Augustine's diagnosis on its head: it was in fact Christianity that had largely undermined the empire, and less so its internal flaws.

Devout Catholic that he was, Tolkien largely adopts Augustine's point of view in diagnosing the decline and fall of the Númenórean empire. In charting the descent of the Númenórean kings from the ideal (Elros) to the perverted (Al-Pharazôn), he clearly shows how power, pride, luxury, and lust for order inevitably give rise to self-destruction and how it is the turning away from true religion that brings about a fall. Gibbon was acutely aware of the resonances between his subject and the ascendent British Empire of the eighteenth century, and Tolkien, too, living at the cusp of its steep decline, must likewise have seen the analogies between his Númenor and Great Britain.

THE BATTLE OF THE GWATHLÓ
MAURO MAZZARA

THE RETURN OF SAURON

Much has been written of the influences that shape Tolkien's depiction of Sauron – the chief antagonist in the history of both the Second and Third Ages. All manner of dark lords and ring lords have been cited as contributing to his character – from outright spirits of evil such as the Christian Satan to more ambivalent figures such as the one-eyed Odin. Even his very name seems to drip malevolence – with its play on the Greek – *sauros* – meaning lizard – and the English near-homophone "sour", evoking the dark bitterness that has long ago twisted Sauron's heart.

Fictionally speaking, Sauron is an altogether more successful antagonist and embodiment of evil than his First Age predecessor and liege lord, Morgoth. While Morgoth – one of the godlike Valar – is too remote and mythological to instil very much fear in the readers of *The Silmarillion*, Sauron, as he appears – or rather looms – in *The Lord of the Rings*, has a more disquieting and disturbing effect, encapsulated in the symbol of the lidless eye worn by his minions. Simultaneously absent and all-pervasive in the novel that bears his name, he seems to become an emanation of the corruption that lurks in the hearts and minds of the huge cast of characters – even those who, ostensibly, oppose him such as Saruman and even some of the best, like Frodo or Galadriel. Significantly, Sauron's return in around the year 500 of the Second Age likewise might be said to coincide with the resurgent corruption of Men, Dwarves and Elves. While narratively (in *Akallabêth*, for example) Sauron acts as the catalyst for this corruption, we might feasibly argue that he is in fact only a projection of actual, pre-existent evil.

In the First Age, Sauron – originally an angelic spirit and follower of the Valar Aulë named Mairon – plays only second fiddle as Morgoth's chief servant. Like many of Morgoth's followers he is a shapeshifter – in the tale of Beren and Lúthien appearing in the guises of serpent, wolf and vampire – an ability that associates him with countless shapeshifting spirits in real-world mythologies. To take just one example, the amoral Norse god Loki on various occasions takes the form of a flea, a salmon and a mare in order to sow mischief and mayhem among the Nine Worlds.

In the Second Age, by contrast, Sauron adopts a more subtle strategy (perhaps having learned from Morgoth's mistakes), assuming a fair form to ensnare the peoples of Middle-earth and thereby trick them into doing his will. Now he appears in the guise of a helper – the angelic Annatar, Lord of Gifts – promising deep knowledge to the Elves and immortality to the Númenóreans. In this new role, he seems to mimic and subvert the trickster figures of mythology, who, acting as culture heroes, bring aspects of civilization to humans that the gods might otherwise have denied them. Prometheus, who steals fire from the gods of Olympus to give to humankind, is the paradigm here – a master artificer whom the fiery Ring-maker Sauron mirrors and distorts.

PART TWO.

THE ELVISH KINGDOMS
AND THE RINGS OF POWER

1 Foundation of Lindon, under Gil-galad

c. 500 Sauron returns to Middle-earth

c. 750 Establishment of Eregion (Hollin) by Celebrimbor

1200 Gil-galad rejects Annatar (Sauron in disguise)

c. 1350 Galadriel and Celeborn settle in Lothlórien

1500 The Elves of Eregion begin to forge the Rings of Power

1590 Celebrimbor forges the Three Rings

1600 Sauron forges the One Ring in Orodruin and completes his fortress, Barad-dûr

1693 Outbreak of the War of the Elves and Sauron

1695 Sauron invades Eriador

1697 Fall of Eregion, death of Celebrimbor; foundation of Imladris (Rivendell)

1699 Sauron overruns Eriador

1701 The First White Council held

THE SACK OF EREGION
MAURO MAZZARA

INTRODUCTION

The Second Age marks the beginning of the slow ascendancy of Men in the history of Middle-earth, as witnessed in the spotlight thrown onto Númenor in Tolkien's account of it. This is the Númenórean age, not an Elvish age of Lindon or Eregion, Elven realms that, though clearly powerful, remain shadowy in comparison to the detailed evocation of this vast island far out in the Belegaer. Likewise, compared to the bewildering plethora of heroic Elves we encounter in *The Silmarillion*, in the Second Age we have only a handful: Gil-galad, Círdan, Celebrimbor, Elrond and Galadriel – and of these only Gil-galad seems to shine as a truly epic figure.

Nonetheless, the history of the Elves of the Second Age is nonetheless crucial, if only because in it Tolkien retrospectively plants the seeds for his two great narratives of the Third Age: *The Lord of the Rings* and *The Hobbit*. While in Númenor Tolkien creates a memorable epic of splendid rise and tragic decline, the key episode of the Second Age – at least in terms of Middle-earth's unfolding history – is the forging of the Rings of Power (bar the One) in a minor Elvish city in an obscure corner of the continent. Big history, Tolkien seems to say, begins in a (ostensibly) small way.

In this section, then, we turn our attention to continental Middle-earth – to its new geography and new (as well as old) realms and to the making of the rings that began in 1500 SA and culminated in the forging of the One Ring in 1600 – the turning point in the history of the age. The primary sources are Appendix B of *The Lord of the Rings* and the fragmentary narratives given in *Unfinished Tales*, most notably the account of "Galadriel and Celeborn".

ERED LUIN
ŠÁRKA ŠKORPÍKOVÁ

AN UNSTABLE GEOLOGY

Arda – the world of which Middle-earth is a part – is notoriously unstable. While our planet Earth has had its own ups and downs through the aeons, its transformation has been, by and large, very, very slow. The "geology" of Arda, by contrast, is dramatic, the changes it undergoes almost crazily rapid. Throughout its history, mountain ranges get thrown over or raised up, seas overwhelm the land, islands rise and fall beneath the waves like yo-yos, and a whole continent (Aman) is removed to another dimension. The Powers of Arda – both the good and evil – are clearly not shy of making big, big changes in their wars and struggles, no matter what the consequences might be or however illogical – geologically speaking – the results.

The first great change in the history of Arda, if we discount the rounds of making and marring that take place in its deepest times, takes place at the end of the First Age, when the greater part of Beleriand – the great homeland of the Elves in Middle-earth – is destroyed during the War of Wrath and then overwhelmed by the Western Sea. The coastline is utterly changed, and the Ered Luin – the Blue Mountains – once hundreds of miles from the sea and forming an unbroken chain that tracked the eastern border of Beleriand – is now broken by the massive Gulf of Lune and is at most only a few dozen miles from Belegaer. The creation of the island of Elenna (Númenor), in the midst of the Great Sea, can hardly be said to make up for such a cataclysmic territorial loss.

Geologists like to make fun of the "unscientific" geology of Arda – the perpendicular sets of mountain chains draw especial criticism and mirth. We might excuse Tolkien's playing fast and loose with geology by pointing out that he was unlikely to have any or very little knowledge of plate tectonics – a science still in its infancy in the 1950s. However, this is to miss the point – a new age and a new struggle demands a new landscape, and Tolkien's marvellously malleable Middle-earth provided this admirably.

LINDON — A NEW REALM

Lindon was the longest enduring of the Elvish realms of Middle-earth, founded by Gil-galad at the very beginning of the Second Age and surviving, even if in ever-diminishing form, until well into the Fourth, with the departure of the last of the Eldar into the West. The country was the last surviving, most easterly fragment of Beleriand – the major part of Ossiriand that was home to a kindred of Nandorin Elves known as the Laiquendi: Green-elves. The name Lindon – "Land of Singers" – was given to the land by the Sindarin because the Green-elves were famous singers; the original name of the Nandorin realm of Lindórinand ("Valley of the Land of Singers", later Lothlórien) likewise referenced their vocal gifts.

The geography of Lindon, cut in two – into Harlindon and Forlindon (North and South Lindon) as it is by the massive Gulf of Lhûn (or Lune), has quite often been likened to the geography of Wales and the West Country, two "Celtic" lands divided by the Bristol Channel. The northward trajectory of the River Lhûn, it is pointed out, also resembles that of the River Severn. Other "evidence" has been cited in support of this theory – Tolkien's conception of Sindarin – the predominant language of both Beleriand and Lindon – was certainly influenced by Welsh, and the people of Wales, of course, are famous singers. Intriguing as these suggestions are, they do not do much to enrich our sense of this enduring but ever-fragile land – which acts, even more than Beleriand before it, as a threshold between two worlds – Middle-earth and Valinor, between this life and that.

ELVES LISTENING TO MINSTREL
VICTOR AMBRUS

GIL-GALAD WITH AEGLOS
MAURO MAZZARA

GIL-GALAD — ARTHURIAN STAR

While Tolkien changed his mind several times about his lineage, Gil-galad is the King of Lindon and the last High King of the Noldor in Middle-earth. In *The Lord of the Rings*, Samwise Gamgee sings the opening verses of "The Fall of Gil-galad" as the Hobbits and Strider/Aragorn make their journey to Weathertop. Sam has been taught the poem by Bilbo Baggins, who has at some point translated the whole of this ancient lay. The subject of song thousands of years after his death, Gil-galad is the towering figure of the Second Age, and as such appears – from the perspective of the late Third Age – suspended between history and myth, rather like the British King Arthur, who similarly loses his life in a final apocalyptic battle. The Arthurian resonances of Gil-galad are sharpened by the resemblance of his name to Galahad – the most perfect knight of Arthur's Round Table and the only one (in most versions) to achieve the Quest of the Holy Grail.

Gil-galad is certainly as close as Tolkien comes to creating the perfect Elvish hero. His name, which is an example of what Tolkien calls an *amilessë*, or "mother-name" – means "Radiant Star" in Sindarin, a name with obvious Christian associations: Christ, as the bringer of hope and redemption, is thrice referred to as the Morning Star in the Bible (2 Peter 1:19; Revelation 2:28 and 22:16). In this light, his death in single combat with Sauron at the Siege of Barad-dûr takes on the character of a Christological struggle between good and evil.

THE KNIGHT
IAN MILLER

MITHLOND — MISTS AND MYTHS

Tolkien is fond of giving his geographic features colourful names: we have, for example, Blue, White, Grey and Red Mountains (Ered Luin in Lindon; Ered Nimrais in Gondor; Ered Mithrin in Rhovanion; and the Orocarni in the far north-east of Middle-earth); we have, of course, Greenwood the Great; and there are rivers, too, with names like Greyflood or Redwater. The features usually get their names from some natural characteristic – Ered Nimrais are so called because of their high peaks that remain snow-capped even in summer; the Redwater gets its name because of the iron deposits that are brought down from the Iron Mountains.

We may perhaps wonder why the port-capital of Lindon, the Grey Havens – or Mithlond in Sindarin – gets its name. On one level, it refers to the Grey-elves who are its primary inhabitants – the Sindar (Quenya for "Grey Ones", Elves who are neither of the Light or the Darkness, but in-between, of the twilight), but it also alludes to the grey of the sea and to the grey veils of mist that separate Middle-earth from Valinor, which draw apart for Frodo at the end of *The Lord of the Rings* (Tolkienian etymologies for the word *mith* related it to both "grey" and "mist").

Related to all these associations is grey as the colour of transition, between light and dark, between states, of change and travel, and the getting of wisdom. Is it a coincidence that Gandalf has the Sindarin name Mithrandir, meaning Grey Pilgrim, and that Gandalf the Grey is the wisest of the Istari, if not all the Maiar?

THE GREY HAVENS
MAURO MAZZARA

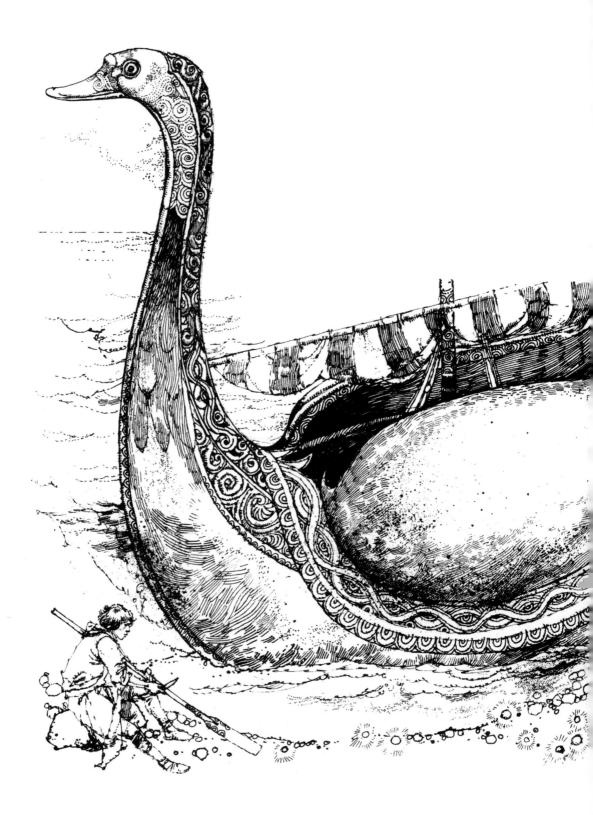

THE BUILDING OF VINGILÓTË
VICTOR AMBRUS

CÍRDAN THE SHIPWRIGHT – INTERMEDIARY BETWEEN WORLDS

Círdan the Shipwright, Master of the Grey Havens and one of the very eldest of the Elves, plays an important role in the unfolding history of Middle-earth down through the ages but nonetheless remains an enigmatic, shadowy figure, and perhaps deliberately so.

Behind his appearance at the elegiac close of *The Lord of the Rings* as the facilitator of Frodo and Bilbo's sailing into the West is a long tradition of his role as a kind of watery gatekeeper between Middle-earth and Valinor, a role that may invite comparison with St Peter, in his role as the keeper of the Pearly Gates. Círdan's role as an intermediary may even explain Tolkien's concern with this figure towards the very end of his life: one of his last notes relating to Middle-earth concerned the Shipwright. Ships and boats have often been associated with life and death – we have only to think of Viking and Anglo-Saxon ship burials (like the one at Sutton Hoo in Suffolk) or, mythologically, of the mortally wounded King Arthur laid out in a boat on his way to be healed in Avalon.

Through the ages, Círdan is shown to be loyal and foresighted – as well as tenacious in the face of the tumultuous events of Middle-earth. As a skilled builder of ships and ports – he passes his knowledge on to the Númenóreans through his friendship with the mariner Vëantur – he bears some comparison with mythological ship-building heroes, such as the biblical patriarch Noah, builder of the Ark – a ship, like Círdan's, associated with salvation.

Given his watery credentials, Círdan's entrustment with the Ring of Fire, Narya, may be surprising, though here once again the Shipwright acts as an intermediary, since he passes the ring on to the Istari Mithrandir (Gandalf) on his arrival in Middle-earth in the Third Age.

EREGION — LAND OF HOLLY

Tolkien was careful to make his Elven realms geographically and botanically distinctive, whether near-mountain-bound like Gondolin or Rivendell, coastal like Lindon, or forested like Doriath or the Woodland Realm of Greenwood the Great. The kingdom of Eregion is perhaps even more unusual: situated in the western lee of the Misty Mountains, and straddling foothills between the Sirannon ("Gate-stream") and the Gwathir/Gwathló (Greyflood), its chief characteristic is the thickets of holly bushes that flourish there in the Second Age. Eregion means simply "Land of Holly", replicated in its Westron name, Hollin.

Tolkien's choice of holly as the defining species of the realm may have something to do with its folkloric reputation for warding off evil – kept in the house it was said to keep goblins at bay – and perhaps for its striking combination of glossy green leaves and intense red berries – both colours associated with nature spirits like elves in European folklore. Holly – still hale and green in the midst of winter – is associated with fertility and immortality, and thus is an apt enough backdrop for any Elven kingdom. Sadly, the realm proves relatively short-lived – founded in 750 SA, by Celebrimbor, or possibly Galadriel and Celeborn, it was destroyed by the forces of Sauron in 1697 SA. When the Fellowship of the Ring pass through the realm towards the end of the Third Age, they find nothing but occasional ruins, and even the holly bushes have vastly reduced in number, though two grow resolutely on either side of the Gates of Durin (the West-gate).

The capital of Eregion, perhaps sited at the confluence of the Glanduin and the Sirannon, is Ost-in-Edhil. The name – meaning "Fortress of the Elves" – seems rather lacklustre for Tolkien, usually so fecund in name-making – perhaps because his history of the realm is itself so sketchy. The city is hugely important nonetheless in the history of Middle-earth, home as it was to the House of the Mírdain – the guild house of the Jewelsmiths of Eregion where all the Rings of Power – save the One – were made. A busy trade route ran, following the course of the Sirannon, from the city to the West-gate of Moria. The close collaboration of the Elves of Eregion and the Dwarves of Moria is almost unparalleled in Tolkien's history of Middle-earth.

ELVEN KINGOMS IN THE SECOND AGE

FORLINDON
Gil-galad

LINDON
founded 1
by Gil-galad

MITHLOND
Círdan

HARLINDON
Galadriel and Celeborn

IMLADRIS
RIVENDELL
founded c. 1697 SA
by Elrond

HOLLIN
EREGION
founded 1350–1697
by Celeborn
and Galadriel
and Celebrimbor

THE
WOODLAND
REALM
GREENWOOD THE GREAT
founded c. 750
by Oropher

LÓRINAND
LÓRIEN
founded c. 750
by Amdír

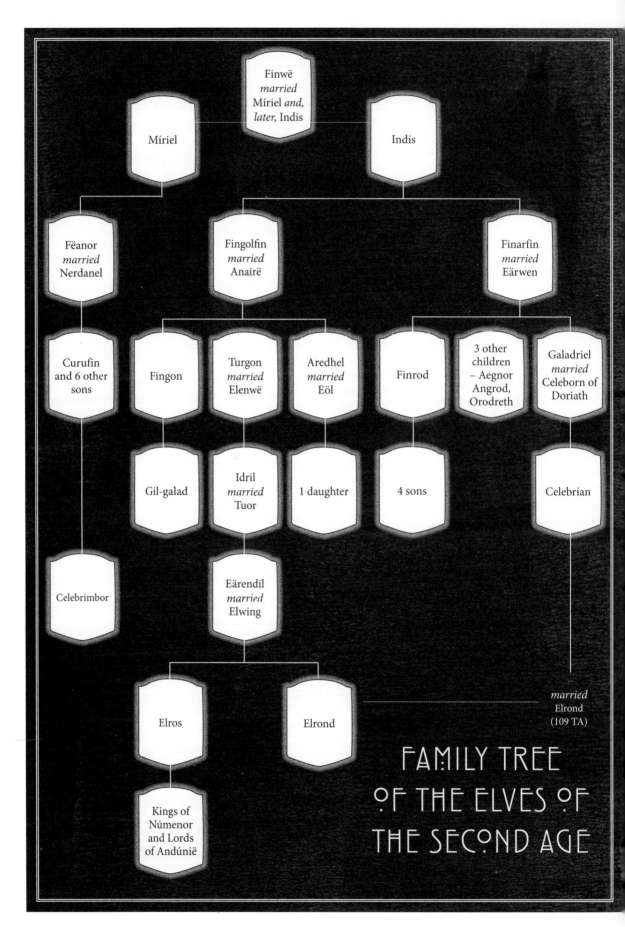

Finwë *married* Míriel *and, later,* Indis

Míriel

Indis

Fëanor *married* Nerdanel

Fingolfin *married* Anairë

Finarfin *married* Eärwen

Curufin and 6 other sons

Fingon

Turgon *married* Elenwë

Aredhel *married* Eöl

Finrod

3 other children – Aegnor Angrod, Orodreth

Galadriel *married* Celeborn of Doriath

Gil-galad

Idril *married* Tuor

1 daughter

4 sons

Celebrían

Celebrimbor

Eärendil *married* Elwing

married Elrond (109 TA)

Elros

Elrond

FAMILY TREE OF THE ELVES OF THE SECOND AGE

Kings of Númenor and Lords of Andúnië

CELEBRIMBOR AT HIS FORGE
VICTOR AMBRUS

CELEBRIMBOR: "SILVER-HAND"

In Tolkien's somewhat unresolved and sketchy history of Eregion, Celebrimbor – the creator of the Three Rings – can appear to be a somewhat pale echo of his grandfather Fëanor, the greatest craftsman of the Elves and the dominant figure in the first half of *The Silmarillion*. There are parallels between the characters: like his grandfather, Celebrimbor is deeply enamoured of craftsmanship, and just as Fëanor is the creator of the Silmarils – the miraculous, hallowed artefacts that become the engines of the tragic history of the First Age – Celebrimbor is the creator of another trio of objects (Vilya, Narya and Nenya) which, along with the One Ring, become the drivers of the later history of the Second and especially the Third Age. A closer reading of *Unfinished Tales* – the most important source of most of our information about Celebrimbor – is suggestive of a rather richer figure. We may regret that Tolkien did not write up the story of the forging of the Rings of Power into a more sustained narrative, as in one of his lays.

The ruler of Eregion is obsessive about his craft – he is described by Tolkien as "almost Dwarvish" in this respect – and his closest friendship appears to be with a Dwarf and fellow craftsman, Narvi, with whom he makes the Doors of Durin, the West-gate of Moria encountered by the Fellowship in *The Lord of the Rings*. (Interestingly, the friendship between Celebrimbor and Narvi seems to foreshadow that between Legolas and Gimli.) Like Fëanor, he seems to have been in part inspired by the figure of Volundr (Wayland the Smith), who in the Poetic Edda is said to have forged gold rings set with gems, much like the Three Rings.

Celebrimbor's Sindarin name means "Silver-Hand", which Tolkien borrowed from an epithet of the Irish hero Nuada, the first king of the Elven-like race known as the Tuatha Dé Danann, although otherwise there are no similarities in their stories. In naming Celebrimbor, Tolkien seems to have been influenced by his work at the Temple of Nodens, although he may have thought it an apt enough name for a master smith and lover of the silvery metal mithril.

HERO AND MARTYR

Celebrimbor appears to be a wiser, less wilful character than Fëanor: he is mistrustful of Annatar/Sauron, forging the Three Rings in secret, and when tortured by Sauron steadfastly refuses to betray the whereabouts of the Elven-rings (even if he reveals the whereabouts of the Seven). Celebrimbor's death by torture and Sauron's use of his body, pierced with arrows and mounted on a pole, as a savage warning to the forces of Lindon, almost raises him to the status of Christian martyr. His transfixed body cannot but remind us of the martyrdom of St Sebastian, the early Christian soldier-saint who, because of his faith, was punished by the emperor Diocletian by being tied to a stake and used for archery practice. The saint miraculously survived to face another martyrdom, but Celebrimbor does not. The image Tolkien creates of the dead Elven-smith is one of the most horrific in his work – perhaps standing in for the author's fallen comrades during the trench warfare of the First World War.

THE DEATH OF CELEBRIMBOR
PETER PRICE

THE WOODLAND REALM
ANDREA PIPARO

THE WOODLAND REALM

The Woodland Realm, in Greenwood the Great, is best known for its important role in *The Hobbit*, where Bilbo and the Dwarves become entangled with its initially mistrustful and overbearing Elvenking. The Elves of *The Hobbit* are rather more ambivalent in their nature than our general impression of their kind in *The Silmarillion* and elsewhere, earthier and more dangerous and more akin to the elves of Norse mythology or English folklore. Tolkien later explained this discrepancy through the development of the complex and long back history for the realm, stretching back to the Years of the Trees. Initially it is the long-standing home of a large number of Teleri Elves who left the Great Journey westwards to Valinor. But at the beginning of the Second Age a Sindarin prince of Doriath named Oropher (the father of Thranduil – the name later given to the Elvenking we meet in *The Hobbit*) leads a group of refugees from Beleriand eastwards and settles in the Woodland Realm, soon after becoming its king.

Oropher's reverse trek through Middle-earth seems to suggest that, after the disaster of Beleriand, the Elves felt a desire for a simpler, more traditional way of life, retracing the path of the Great Journey. This retrograde movement is paralleled by that of Galadriel and Celeborn who similarly become rulers of a what we might call a neo-traditionalist community – drawing together both the Elves of Beleriand and the Nandor – this time in Lothlórien. The imposition of Sindarin or Noldorin rule on Nandorin populations may strike us as colonialist, though it's unlikely Tolkien saw it in this way.

PEOPLE OF THE TREES

The rulers of the Woodland Realm all have appropriately leafy names: Oropher means "tall beech tree", Thranduil "vigorous spring", and the latter's son, Legolas – one of the lead characters in *The Lord of the Rings* – is simply "Greenleaf".

In European folklore the association of elves with forests and woodlands, as well as with the mysterious grey hours around twilight, is an old one. In Germanic folklore there are the Moosleute ("moss people"), an elven folk associated with the great forests that once covered much of Europe and considered by humans as both dangerous and potentially beneficial (the Men of Beleriand have similar beliefs about the Grey Elves and the enchantments of Doriath). The sylvan association continued into early modern times, as we see in the fairies of William Shakespeare's *A Midsummer Night's Dream* (1595–6). There, in the king and queen of the fairies, Oberon and Titania, we may see a buried inspiration for King Thingol and Queen Melian.

LOTHLÓRIEN
PETER PRICE

LINDÓRINAND / LOTHLÓRIEN

In *The Lord of the Rings* Lothlórien – the woodland realm of Galadriel and Celeborn – is tucked in an angle of land between the Great River and its tributary the Silverlode, not far east of the Misty Mountains – in an idyllic Elven otherworld that exists beyond the usual flow of time. As usual, Tolkien's inspirations are rich and varied – the Ljósálfheimr (Home of the Light-elves) of Norse cosmology; the Elfhome of medieval legend (notably in the tales about the poet Thomas the Rhymer), into which mortals wander at their peril (as the Rohirrim would have it); and the strange otherworlds of Welsh and Irish myths that are often reached by crossing water, just as the Fellowship must cross water to reach Lothlórien.

The Lothlórien of the Third Age is, however – as Tolkien makes clear in the realm's evolving but infuriatingly similar names – very much the fabrication of Galadriel and the power of her ring, Nenya. The realm began its life very much like the Woodland Realm, just across the Great River, as the home of Nandorin Elves – and in the early Second Age was still known by its Nandorin name – Lindórinand, meaning "Valley of the Land of the Singers". After Galadriel plants the golden mallorn trees, it becomes alternatively Lórinand (Nandorin for "Valley of Gold") and Laurelindórenan ("Valley of Singing Gold") and finally – in its most Galadriel-ized avatar, Lothlórien ("Dream Flower") or simply Lórien ("Dreamland"), the undoubtedly playful name changes suggesting the realm's gradual retreat from the chronological and geographical boundaries of the real Middle-earth.

We should imagine the Lindórinand of the early Second Age at least as a rather more prosaic place than its Third Age successor (a reversal of, or – perhaps better – exception to, the normal course of Middle-earth history where the world is progressively disenchanted as the Elves' power diminishes) – still beautiful and pristine, of course, but not yet subject to the Noldorin queen's powerful enchantments. Like the Woodland Realm, its Nandor-majority population is initially ruled by a Sindarin refugee from Doriath in Beleriand – Amdír – so that we might well imagine Oropher and Amdír making the eastward trek together and dividing up the land, conquistador-style.

GALADRIEL — LADY OF THE GOLDEN WOOD

Galadriel was a Noldor noblewoman, only daughter of Finarfin, and, in *The Lord of the Rings*, the ruler of the enchanted Elven realm of Lothlórien, "the land of blossoms dreaming". In that hidden wooded land, robed in white and golden-haired, she commands great powers of enchantment and prophecy.

In ancient Welsh mythology we find forest and water nymphs who closely resemble Galadriel, the guardians of sacred fountains, wells and grottoes hidden in deep forest vales. Like Tolkien's "Lady of Light", White Ladies have eyes like stars and bodies that shimmer with light, betokening their close affinity with the starlit night. To reach their realms it is commonly necessary to pass through or across water that was – as is said when the Fellowship cross over a river into Lothlórien – "like crossing a bridge in time". These White Ladies often lived in realms "outside of time" in crystal palaces beneath water or floating in air, all glowing with silver and golden light.

In Arthurian tradition, Vivien the Lady of the Lake – perhaps in origin a Celtic White Lady herself – rises dressed in white from her palace beneath the lake to present the sword and scabbard of Excalibur to the rightful king. Vivien also raises Lancelot du Lac, before sending him into the world with the arms of war. We might see a similar figure in Greek mythology, the sea nymph Thetis, mother of Achilles, the greatest hero of the Trojan War, who gifts her son with his armour.

Across cultures and times we find water and forest deities who give protection, prophecies, inspiration, invisibility and strength to their protégés. Galadriel, too, belongs to this tradition, presiding over a realm of dreams and desires, visions and illusions, gifts and blessings.

In *The Lord of the Rings* Galadriel makes a deep impression. This is in part due to the fact that Tolkien shows us the Lady of Lothlórien through the eyes of the Hobbits, especially Frodo, who witnesses her brief transformation, when tempted by the One Ring, into a "Dark Queen". It is also because, so far, the book has been so male-dominated, with only rare and fleeting appearances by female characters – the occasional Hobbit, Goldberry and Arwen. The appearance of this powerful, preternaturally female character comes almost like a shock to the system for the reader, who has become acculturated to the homosocial world that Tolkien has created.

The powerful presence of Galadriel in *The Lord of the Rings* clearly presented Tolkien with a problem when he came to developing a suitable backstory that linked her to the Elven history of the First and Second Ages: how did this clearly high-ranking High Elven Lady end up in the "backwoods" of Lothlórien at all? When did she meet her husband, Celeborn? Why did she not return to Valinor at the end of the First Age like most of her surviving kin? As Tolkien's son and literary executor, Christopher Tolkien, painstakingly showed in his account in *Unfinished Tales*, the author devoted numerous notes to the issue over the years, as he puzzled things through, and as Galadriel's story went through countless permutations as he tried first one solution then another. The story as given in *The Silmarillion* is only a midway snapshot, and it could be argued that the "problem" of Galadriel was never quite (re)solved to Tolkien's satisfaction.

GALADRIEL
MAURO MAZZARA

A RESTLESS SPIRIT

The early Galadriel, as portrayed in *The Silmarillion*, is restless and ambitious, like many of her Noldor kinsfolk (she is, after all, the niece of Fëanor, even if she mistrusts him). She participates in the revolt of the Noldor against the Valar, we are told, because she wishes to rule on her own account in Middle-earth, but not in the Kinslaying that leads to the ban on many of her people returning to Valinor. While Tolkien toned down her wilfulness and waywardness in later iterations, the same restlessness is evident in her history through the Second Age, where she rules first a fief in Lindon, then founds, with Celeborn, a new Noldorin realm in Eregion and finally settles in the Nandorin realm of Lindórinand (Lothlórien-to-be) east of the Misty Mountains, eventually becoming its Lady alongside her Lord. Tolkien also eventually decided that Galadriel met her husband not in Lothlórien but in Doriath and that he was Sindarin, not Nandorin – a decision that ties her to a husband, almost her equal, from early on and diminishes our sense of her as a free agent, or even a loose cannon.

Perhaps Tolkien's trouble with Galadriel can be explained by his trouble with powerful women in general. A man of his times, he believed, as his letters show, that women were above all instinctive, driven by a desire to serve (men), and yet in Galadriel he created an Elven queen who seems, even against her creator's will, to resist such stereotyping and whose husband always appears rather shadowy and inconsequential beside her, however much she defers to him on the page.

IMLADRIS / RIVENDELL

Founded by Elrond in the aftermath of the War of Sauron and the Elves in 1687 SA, Rivendell (Imladris in Sindarin) is the last created realm of the Eldar in Middle-earth, and plays only a marginal role in the events of the Second Age, most significantly serving as a staging camp for the forces of Gil-galad and Elendil before the Battle of Dagorlad.

Tolkien is rather hazy about the nature of Imladris – is it fortress, town, village or extended house (in *The Hobbit* it is cumbrously nicknamed the "Last Homely House East of the Sea")? In its hidden, secluded setting it seems to echo the hidden city of Gondolin in Beleriand, though on a much diminished scale. In *The Lord of the Rings*, Elrond insists that Rivendell is a haven of peace and Elven-lore rather than a stronghold, although its identity of course could have developed over its long history.

As ever, a whole cluster of inspirations lie behind this hidden place. Of these, Tolkien's 1911 hike through the idyllic Swiss valley of Lauterbrunnental was undoubtedly the most formative – Tolkien's youthful drawings of Lauterbrunnental clearly inspired his later depictions of Rivendell, both written and visual, and there are certain verbal plays: the River Brunnen, meaning Loudwater, which helps protect the Hidden Valley, clearly refers to the Lauterbrunnen (Loud Spring) of the Swiss valley.

RIVENDELL
MELVYN GRANT

RIVENDELL — ELVES AND OXFORD DONS

Viewing the north-west of Middle-earth as equivalent in latitude to the coastline of Europe and the north shore of the Mediterranean, Tolkien suggests that: "Hobbiton and Rivendell are taken (as intended) to be at about the latitude of Oxford." Tolkien has informed us that the Shire is analogous to rural Warwickshire; Lindon, to Wales and Cornwall. It is quite clear that Rivendell is not just "on the latitude of Oxford", it is an analogy for Oxford as well. Rivendell was an Elvish Oxford, and Oxford during the Great War soon became very like a human Rivendell: a refuge, a house of lore and good counsel in the midst of a world gone mad with slaughter and war. For Tolkien, Oxford was just such a refuge. In fact, that world of slaughter in the Great War nearly consumed Tolkien, as it had consumed almost all of his contemporaries. Ironically, had Tolkien not become violently ill with the debilitating illness known as "trench fever" he probably would not have survived the conflict. A century before Tolkien's remarks above, the poet Matthew Arnold saw Oxford in the same way: "Oxford, the Oxford of the past, has many faults; and she has paid heavily for them in defeat, in isolation, in want of hold upon the modern world. Yet we in Oxford brought up amidst the beauty and sweetness of that beautiful place, have not failed to seize one truth – the truth that beauty and sweetness are essential characters of a complete human perfection." Matthew Arnold's statement, with a few minor adjustments, could almost be an Elvish manifesto of an eternal creative drive toward perfection.

IMLADRIS — THE ELVISH DELPHI

Rivendell was not only a safe refuge; like Oxford it was a place of learning and long meditation for the world-weary. Rivendell was a house where scribes and scholars might work in peace. In Rivendell, the common tongue was Westron; while the true scholar's choice was the ancient Elvish languages of Sindarin and Quenya. In Oxford, the common tongue was English; while the true scholar's choices were the ancient languages of Latin and Greek. In both of these closed societies, languages were immediate and effective "indicators of social class and distinction". Oxford society, just like Rivendell's, was willfully "out of time" with the contemporary world. Master Elrond's use of language was archaic, but not excessively so for someone 6,000 years old. Since the early nineteenth century Oxford has been, rather magnificently, entitled the "Home of Lost Causes".

There was something else about Rivendell. Something best viewed through examining the word "Imladris", not just its Elvish name, but an alternate reality; something "other", that concerns itself with the Elvish aspects of second sight, prophetic dreams, and waking visions. This House of Lore not only kept historic artefacts and documents; Master Elrond the Half-elven was himself a living history – six millennia of it. In Imladris, Elrond Half-elven was perhaps best consulted as an ancient living oracle. Tolkien often leaves clues in names: Rivendell's Westron name "Karningul" meaning "Cleft Valley" is repeated in its Sindarin name "Imladris" which means "Deep Cleft Dale" because it is in a hidden rock cleft at the foot of a pass in the Misty Mountains. This location kept Imladris hidden by natural illusions created by the folds in the rock face of the deep-cut valley. This hidden cleft of darkness was also an allusion – in reverse – to a most revealing Cleft of Light in the immortal kingdom of Eldamar. This was the Calacirya, the "Cleft of the Valley of Light", the only pass through the Pelóri Mountains which encircle the Undying Lands. This was the Cleft of Light that allowed the Light of the Trees of the Valar to shine out upon Eldamar.

In ancient Greece, there was another sacred "Cleft of Light". This was the Oracle at Delphi that was built in a narrow pass through the mountains of Parnassus, sacred to the sun god Apollo. Delphi means "cleft" in Greek. All the masters of the ancient world came to consult the Oracle at Delphi. The treasures of many cities and the archives of Delphi were protected within this sanctuary by treaty or diplomatic agreement, and to some degree by fear of Apollo's wrath. Like Imladris, Delphi was believed to be under the protection of the river and mountain spirits around it. In *The Lord of the Rings*, an invasion of Imladris is attempted by Ringwraiths, but this was rapidly repelled when the river rose in a mighty flood that swept the demonic horsemen away. Similarly, ancient historians tell of the Persian King Xerxes who, upon invading Greece, ordered his bodyguard to march on the unfortified sanctuary of Delphi. In this attempt, the Persians were utterly destroyed. Their forces were swept away by a thunderous series of flash floods, followed by a massive crush of landslides that blocked the mountain passes and brought an end to the invasion. The temple of Apollo was the house of record, law and lore. It was also the house of consultation before any great adventure or campaign. Its prophecies were most often double edged, and as such a warning and a caution to the proud and the mighty. The future was not fixed, but determined by personal courage and will.

Written across the entrance to Apollo's temple was written "Know thyself". Delphi and Imladris were places where the inner journey was encouraged, before the outer journey was taken in good faith. Delphi and Imladris were both places where fellowships were created and journeys begun. These are refuges from which adventurers set out upon the wide world with hope, and a sign of good fortune.

RIVENDELL
ANDREA PIPARO

KHAZAD-DÛM

The Elvish realms of Middle-earth were not the only kingdoms of the Second Age. The Dwarf-kingdom of Khazad-dûm ("Delving of the Dwarves") was another Second Age "super-power", although more marginal its effects on the course of its history. Founded by the Father of the Longbeard Dwarves, Durin I, during the Years of the Trees (that is, before the creation of the Sun and the Moon), Khazad-dûm was already a great kingdom in the First Age, but reached a new ascendancy in the Second, with the arrival of refugees from the Dwarven cities of Beleriand, Belegost and Nogrod, and through its later collaboration with the Elven realm of Eregion.

Tolkien's imagining of Khazad-dûm, famed for its magnificent subterranean architecture of halls, bridges and staircases, was coloured by the Nidavellir ("Dark Fields") or Svartalfheim ("Black Elf Home") of Norse mythology, one of the Nine Worlds – a subterranean land of mines, forges and mead-halls. The name for Khazad-dûm after its abandonment in the Third Age, Moria ("Dark Pit"), underscores this connection with the Norse world of dwarves.

DWARVES
IAN MILLER

DWARVES IN THE SEC°ND AGE

If our only knowledge of the Dwarves was founded solely on our reading of *The Hobbit*, or even *The Lord of the Rings*, we might be surprised by their larger cultural reputation through the ages of Middle-earth as a secretive, insular people whose greed for gold and knowledge and their somewhat amoral approach to the affairs of the world make them at least uncertain, if not untrustworthy, partners in the wider struggle against evil. Of course, there are elements of this character in *The Hobbit*, but the overall impression given by Thorin and Company is of jovial heartiness and dogged loyalty, and even their faults – most notably, greediness – are cast in comic vein, as we see in the "Unexpected Party" and their remorseless raiding of Bilbo's multiple larders.

THE DWARVEN CITY
ROBERT ZIG°

THE DWARF
ANDREW MOCKETT

THE INSULARITY OF DWARVES

Of course, we might explain the discrepancy by pointing to the fact that *The Hobbit* is metafictionally based on Bilbo's own account of his adventures – *There and Back Again* – as preserved in the *Red Book of Westmarch* and that we are in some sense looking at the Dwarves through his sympathetic eyes. Much the same might apply to *The Lord of the Rings*, which is based on Frodo's account of his quest and influenced by his friendship with the almost entirely amiable, if slightly irascible, Dwarf Gimli.

By contrast, Tolkien implies that the earlier history of the Middle-earth Dwarves (especially through the First and Second Ages) comes to us through Elvish recordkeeping and Elvish chroniclers. The Elves were mistrustful of the Dwarves and were perhaps prejudiced in their portrayal of them and their role. How different, we may wonder, the history of Middle-earth might be if it were told from a Dwarvish perspective – from the viewpoint of the mountains, rather than of the forest, so to speak?

As it is, the insularity of the Dwarves is expressed in their very creation – the Vala Aulë forms the Seven Fathers of the Dwarves in secret, without Ilúvatar's and the Valar's knowing. If we were especially blinkered Elves, we might even see the creation of the Dwarves as analogous to the breeding of the Orcs and other monstrous beings by Morgoth, Sauron and Saruman, creatures made out of pride and without divine sanction (although Aulë is soon granted this for his "children", the Dwarves). Above all, though, the Dwarves are portrayed as morally "neutral", their characters summed up neatly in the phrase we find in *The Silmarillion:* "stone-hard, stubborn, fast in friendship and in enmity".

The depiction of the Dwarves in the tales of the First Age – concerning their role in the history of Beleriand – is deeply ambivalent, perhaps under the influence of the near-malevolent character of their namesakes in Norse mythology – which was undoubtedly the biggest inspiration for Tolkien's depiction of the events of the First Age. While they are occasionally shown to be allies of the Elves of Beleriand, helping to build their cities and fighting against the forces of Morgoth, it is their greed that is their paramount characteristic. In their lust to repossess the fabulous necklace Nauglamír, the Dwarves of Nogrod (a city in the bowels of the Blue Mountains) slay the Sindarin king of Doriath, Thingol, and, in the following Elvish–Dwarvish feud, sack Menegroth, Doriath's capital.

A NEW GOLDEN AGE

Despite this dark history of greed and feuding, the Second Age holds out hope for an alternative relationship between Elves and Dwarves and a more positive character of the Dwarves more generally. After the destruction of Beleriand and, along with it, the ruin of the Dwarvish kingdoms of Nogrod and Belegost, the vast majority of the Dwarves migrate eastwards to the greatest city of the Dwarves, Khazad-dûm (Moria), heralding the rapid expansion and cultural zenith of this most ancient of Dwarvish cities under Durin III.

The foundation of the Elvish kingdom of Eregion in the shadow of the Misty Mountains, adjacent to Khazad-dûm, fosters a new collaboration between Elves and Dwarves, as equal partners. Mistrust turns to collaboration – as evidenced by the close friendship between two master smiths, the Elf Celebrimbor and the Dwarf Narvi – and greed becomes a mutually beneficial trading relationship, materialized in the road that runs between Eregion's capital, Ost-in-Edhil, and the West-gate of Khazad-dûm, the so-called Doors of Durin. The gate itself and its inscription "Speak friend and enter" – created by Celebrimbor and the Dwarf Narvi to facilitate communications and trade between their two peoples – symbolizes the new spirit. That two of the Fellowship who encounter the door in the Third Age are the initially mistrustful pair, the Elf Legolas and Dwarf Gimli, foreshadows their blossoming friendship and the revival of the promise laid out by Eregion–Khazad-dûm relations in the Fourth Age. The Dwarves of Khazad-dûm play a decisive role in the war between the Elves and Sauron, their surprise attack on Sauron's forces from the rear enabling Elrond and the forces of Lindon to make good their escape northwards. The destruction of Eregion signals a new period of splendid isolation for the kingdom but also a slow decline.

DWARVES AS RING-BEARERS

There were Seven Dwarf-Rings to match the Seven Fathers. Tolkien never quite resolved how the Dwarves came into possession of the rings. In one version (let's call it the Dwarvish version), Celebrimbor gives the first of the Seven directly to Durin III, which eventually is named the Ring of Thrór after one of its bearers. In another version – less flattering to the Dwarves – Celebrimbor reveals the whereabouts of the Seven to Sauron under torture and Sauron subsequently gifts the rings to various Dwarven rulers (thereby suggesting that they had ongoing dealings with him).

However they come into possession of the Seven, the Dwarven ring-bearers do not succumb to Sauron in the same way as the Ringwraiths – their stony character protects them. The implication, however, is that the rings do accentuate the Dwarves' more negative characteristics (i.e. their greed for gold and power) throughout the following millennia, and become the basis of their fantastically impressive treasure hordes. This was the fate of the Ring of Thrór, which in the Third Age became the basis of the power and wealth of the Dwarf-kingdom of Erebor – the "Lonely Mountain" of *The Hobbit*.

MORDOR

Even if the peoples of Middle-earth superstitiously avoided mentioning the name of Sauron's evil land, any survey of the realms of the Second Age of Middle-earth would not be complete without a discussion of Mordor. The name is one Tolkien's most ingenious. Even if we knew nothing of Tolkien's fictional world, we would guess that nothing good ever came out of Mordor. The play on the syllable "mor", suggestive of Latin *mortem* and French *mort* – both meaning death – and the numerous English words derived from these roots (mortuary, morbid, etc.); the near-homophonic "murder" involving the switch of the repeated vowel sound; and the rhyming syllables – *mor-dor* – that seem to toll like a death knell – all work together to create a fell-sounding place no one would be in hurry to visit. No one would book a vacation in Mordor.

A quick check of the map and Mordor even looks evil cartographically, surrounded as it is on three sides by suspiciously rectilinear, wall-like mountains (apparently a scar left by the workings of Morgoth early in Arda's history). Mordor is a place apart and, given its sometime active volcano – Orodruin (Mount Doom) – and the surrounding black volcanic plain (Gorgoroth) that are its dominant features, had more than earned its name, meaning "Black Land" (or "Shadow Land"), long before Sauron had even set up his power base here, in 1000 SA.

SHADOW LAND

PETER PRICE

THERE NOT BE DRAGONS

One of the glories of Tolkien's narrative world is his reinvention, or reclamation, of the medieval dragons of Norse and Anglo-Saxon legend. They loom large in two of his major published fictions, *The Silmarillion* and *The Hobbit* – covering the First Age and a short period towards the end of the Third Age, respectively – but are almost entirely absent from his largely fragmentary or synoptic accounts of the Second Age (as well as from *The Lord of the Rings*, it has to be said). To our disappointment, perhaps, we find no equivalent, in the Second Age, of the magnificently malevolent Glaurung – the Father of Dragons who haunts Beleriand and who finally dies at the hand of Túrin, in a re-creation of the titanic struggle between the Germanic hero Siegfried/Sigurd and the dragon Fafnir; nor of Smaug the Golden, sitting atop his vast treasure under the Lonely Mountain, whose riddling humour and dark cunning threaten to steal the stage in the later chapters of *The Hobbit*.

The near utter absence of dragons is largely explicable, of course: they simply have no place in the story or the geography of Númenor – whose rise and fall is the dominant narrative of the Second Age. Perhaps more surprising is the absence of dragons in Tolkien's brief accounts of the War of the Last Alliance, when we might well have surmised that Sauron would have deployed these deadly creatures against his foes. Tolkien's failure to mention them does not mean that they did not take part, of course (if we can be forgiven this epistemological cul-de-sac). The answer is that, narratively speaking, at this point in his history of the Middle-earth, Tolkien had no need for a dragon to act as antagonist – the all-important conflict here is between Gil-galad and Sauron, the two great personifications of good and evil.

Let us content ourselves with imagining, during those long years of the Second Age, the dragons prowling the Withered Heath in the far north of Middle-earth, biding their time until the Third Age, when once again they will rain down mayhem and destruction on the peoples of Middle-earth.

DRAGON

IAN MILLER

SAURON FORGING THE ONE RING
KIP RASMUSSEN

FORGING A BACKSTORY: THE RINGS OF POWER

Tolkien once described how the discovery of the One Ring in an Orc cavern by Bilbo Baggins was as much a surprise to him as it was to his Hobbit hero, knowing, at the time, as little of its history as Bilbo Baggins did. Tolkien has previously explained how it grew from a simple vehicle of plot in *The Hobbit* into the central image of his epic tale *The Lord of the Rings*.

So just how did this incredibly important ring emerge so casually from the caverns of Tolkien's mind, with little to no indication of how significant a symbol it would become in, arguably, one of the greatest fantasy stories ever told? To more fully understand this, it is important to first consider the tradition of a type of storytelling referred to as "ring quest tales". The term is a self-explanatory one and refers to a tale or story with the symbol of the ring at its centre. Such tales are an ancient form of storytelling that are thought to date back to a time before the pyramids of Egypt were built or the walls of Babylon were raised. While the glorious civilization of Greece and the mighty empire of Rome rose and fell, the tradition of ring quest tales lived on, surviving the fall of the pagan gods, and the rise of Muhammad and Christ.

We can garner a rough idea of the early forms the ring quest took from observations made of the nomadic tribes of Lappland and Siberia in the twentieth century, among whom symbolic rituals of the quest still remained intact. Anthropologists living among the shamanic Lapplanders during the last century have frequently recorded the ritual enactment of the ring quest. In this ceremony the shaman or wizard of the tribe places a brass ring on the head of a sacred drum. The designs and markings on the skin of the drum are essentially a cosmic map of the human and spirit worlds. The shaman begins to chant and gently tap the rim of the drumhead with his drum hammer, making the ring move and dance. The ring's progress can be likened to the journey of the human soul, and as it moves around the cosmic map, the shaman sings the tale of the soul's perilous journey through the human and spirit worlds.

Though the bookish Oxford don who was J. R. R. Tolkien and the nomadic, tribal shaman may seem worlds apart, they are intrinsically linked by the single tradition of ring quest tales that span more than 5,000 years. In producing a final typescript for his publisher, Tolkien tapping on his typewriter keys set the wandering soul of his Hobbit hero on a journey that moved and danced to a pulse akin to that tapped out by the shaman on his drum. And the journey of Tolkien's One Ring across the map of Middle-earth is not so unlike the journey of the shaman's ring across the drum map of his human and spirit worlds.

SETTING THE STAGE

It is also important to consider the significance of myth when tracing the inspiration behind Tolkien's One Ring. The richness of this heritage is evident in his tales and his vast mythological structures. Tolkien was deeply committed to the study of the ancient wisdom of the human soul as preserved in myth and legend. In *The Lord of the Rings*, he awoke something deep in human consciousness through the universal language of mythic images drawn from the early history of humankind. His extraordinary tale confirms his place as one of the greatest heirs to an ancient storytelling tradition rooted in a shared symbolic language of myth.

This was one of the most profound aspects of Tolkien's genius as an author. He combined a natural storyteller's ability and inventiveness with a scholar's capacity to draw from the deep well of myth, legend, literature and history. He breathed life into ancient traditions that, but for him, would have remained forever unknown to the large majority of modern readers.

However, it should never be thought that Tolkien's creative process was a mere cobbling together of ancient lore. Richer and more profound though Tolkien's writing is for the ancient tradition it draws upon, Tolkien's art is by no means mere imitation. *The Lord of the Rings* is a highly realized and originally conceived novel that has renewed, invigorated and finally reinvented the ring quest for the twentieth and twenty-first centuries.

The forging of the Rings of Power is perhaps the clearest example of the way in which Tolkien retrospectively uses the Second Age as a way to set the stage for the events that take place in the Third, as related in *The Lord of the Rings* and *The Hobbit*. The little ring that Bilbo "steals" from Gollum in *The Hobbit* serves as not much more than a plot device – enabling the book's emergent hero to practise his craft of burglary and get himself and his companions out of scrapes. In *The Lord of the Rings*, Tolkien not only infinitely magnified the power of the Ring but gave it and its companions, in the form of the Three and the Nine (the Seven play no role), a vastly inflated significance, and to do so sketched out a history that stretches back thousands of years, deep into the Second Age. Gandalf's investigations into the nature of Bilbo's ring, at the beginning of *The Lord of the Rings*, in a way stand in, metafictionally, for Tolkien's own development of the One Ring's power and deep history.

Of course, Tolkien was unable to give anything but a brief (and sometimes contradictory) account of the forging of the Rings. He nonetheless gives what is essentially a foundational myth or myth of origin a distinct and evocative flavour, largely by imbuing it with Norse motifs: in the forging of the Rings of Power in Eregion by the Elf Celebrimbor and Annatar/Sauron, Tolkien brings together magical rings, a Loki-like trickster figure and oddly dwarfish Elves.

ANNATAR — LORD OF GIFTS
ŠÁRKA ŠKORPÍKOVÁ

SAURON AND LOKI

Sauron's role is perhaps the most Norse feature of the tale of the forging of the Rings of Power and is worth exploring in more detail. As Annatar, he comes to the Elves in the guise of a hero – a divine or semi-divine figure found in many mythologies and cultures who offers humankind secret divine knowledge. The god Loki often plays this role in Norse mythology and has sometimes even been seen as a kind of Nordic Prometheus, the Greek Titan who steals fire from the gods and gives it to humanity. Annatar/Sauron's gift to the Elves also involves fire and secret knowledge – here the making of magic rings. However, just as Loki also has a treacherous side – he frequently plots the humiliation of the gods and ultimately engineers their downfall – so, too, does Sauron set out to ensnare the Elves and overturn the status quo of the Valar by means of his poisoned gifts.

When Sauron appears among the Elves of Eregion in the guise of an angelic emissary from the Valar, he gives himself the name Annatar, meaning "Lord of Gifts". Tolkien seems to be making an allusion here to the Anglo-Saxon culture of gift giving from lord to followers, which helped cement bonds of community, loyalty and mutuality. Such gifts most often took the form of food and drink in the mead hall, but also occasionally arm rings of varying degrees of value. Sauron, as we know, wishes to appear as a benefactor, offering the gift of knowledge of ring-making to the Elven-smiths, and thus the name is apposite.

Of course, Sauron's secret aim is not to foster community but to dominate and pervert, and there may likewise be a hint of this in his soubriquet. As a "ring-giver" – an Anglo-Saxon kenning for a king or lord – he is effectively staking his claim as ruler over Middle-earth. Moreover, the Anglo-Saxon and Old High German word *gift* was used not only in the sense of "present" but also as a euphemism for poison – a sense still preserved in the modern German *gift*. Here, Tolkien the philologist may be making a playful reference to Annatar/Sauron as a poisoner of community and to the rings themselves as fatal gifts.

ELVEN-SMITHS

Tolkien's depiction of the Elves as smiths – the Gwaith-i-Mírdain ("People of the Jewel-smiths") – in the story of the forging of the Rings may surprise, given the more traditional association of smithing with underground-dwelling dwarves. Once again, however, Tolkien is drawing on Norse mythology where the division between elves and dwarves is not always that clear-cut. Unlike the Ljósálfar, the light elves, the svartálfar, or dark elves, live underground like dwarves and like them were greedy for gold and jewels and were expert smiths (it may be that the dark elves and dwarves were merely interchangeable). Elves, whether light or dark, are also depicted as smiths in several stories: the so-called Sons of Ivaldi, who make a series of magical artefacts for the gods, are the brothers of the goddess Idunn, who is sometimes described as an elf; while the most famous smith of all, Wayland or, in old Norse, Vǫlundr, is also identified as elven.

Such stories undoubtedly influenced Tolkien's conception of one of the kindreds of Elves described in *The Silmarillion*, the Noldor, whose Quenya name means "The Deep Ones" or "Knowledgeable Ones". In Valinor, they were especially close to the Vala Aulë – the creator of the Dwarves – and under his tutelage became craftspeople of great skill. The greatest of the Noldor and the greatest Elven smith is Fëanor, the maker of the Silmarils, a figure clearly inspired by Wayland. Like Wayland, Fëanor is deeply flawed, filled with pride and wilfulness, and capable of acts of great brutality.

The Noldorin Elves of Eregion, led by Fëanor's grandson Celebrimbor, continued the crafting traditions of their kindred and worked in close collaboration with the Dwarven smiths of Khazad-dûm. While throughout his stories Tolkien makes great play of the ancient enmity between Elves and Dwarves, the story of Eregion and the forging of the rings – encapsulated in the friendship between the Elf Celebrimbor and the Dwarf Narvi – points back to their deep-rooted affinities in Norse mythology.

DWARVEN SMITH
TURNER MOHAN

←———⊰

THE ART OF THE SMITH

The secret of the ring is in its making. To make a ring, one must have the knowledge to smelt and forge metal. The "secret language" of the smith – symbolized by the ring – was his knowledge of metallurgy. Ultimately, this is concerned with the secret of the smelting and forging of iron, which is believed to have been discovered around 1000 BCE in the region of the Caucasus Mountains. It was the atomic secret of its day, a secret that was closely guarded: where the ore was mined, how the metal was extracted, how it was forged into weapons and tools. The smith's extraordinary skill must have seemed reminiscent of the practise of alchemy in that such knowledge must have been perceived as somewhat magical or otherworldly. Because of alchemists' seemingly magical practises, they were often executed as sorcerers or magicians. We will look at the significance of alchemy later on.

Those who possessed the secret of the smith conquered and often exterminated those who did not. The Iron Age transformed nations of timid shepherds and farmers into ferocious warriors capable of catastrophic feats of destruction on their once-powerful, and now-subjugated, neighbours. The hero who won the smith's – or the alchemist's – "ring" in the form of the secret of iron-smelting literally saved his nation.

The arts of the smith and the occult sciences are overlapping techniques handed down as trade secrets with their own rites and rituals. The mysteries of initiation rites and the secret language of the rituals of the trade became symbols in mythic tales.

It is not commonly recognized how profound an impact the rituals and rites of metallurgy have had on myth. However, it is not so much the techniques of metallurgy that are conveyed in these myths, but the secret rituals of initiation into those cults and the spiritual rites practised within the guild, which evolve into the symbols of myth. The symbolic language of the ring quest, at its most profound, is concerned with the "spiritual" consequences of the Bronze and Iron Ages, which changed forever the human condition and perception of the world. Mircea Eliade emphasizes this point: "Before changing the face of the world the Iron Age engendered a large number of rites, myths and symbols which have reverberated throughout the spiritual history of humanity."

The smith was a much revered figure in many cultures but also equally feared, both as the possessor of secret or magical knowledge and as the creator of weapons of violence. The archetypal figure here is perhaps the Anglo-Saxon Wayland the Smith (the Norse Volundr), who in various tales such as the Norse Völundarkviða is depicted as deeply ambivalent – weird and dark. The maker of beguilingly beautiful magic rings and powerful weapons (notably the sword Gram), he is also capable of murder and rape. The figure was an important influence not only on Tolkien's flawed hero Fëanor as well as the altogether more benign figure of Celebrimbor, both of whom are master smiths, but also on Sauron himself, who was originally the Maiar servant of Aulë, the smith of the Valar. As Annatar, Sauron imparts his secret smithing knowledge to the Elven-smiths of Eregion, but with murder and mayhem in his heart.

If one looks at the ring quest myths of most cultures, there are certain constants for the hero in his pursuit of the ring: the magician, the smith, the warrior, the sword, the dwarf, the maiden, the treasure and the dragon. These all relate originally to the rites and processes of metallurgy, and later to the symbolic "secret language" of the alchemist's ring.

In *The Lord of the Rings* Tolkien has all the elements of the ring quest, and yet something wholly original in his own War of the Ring.

NAMING AND NOT NAMING

In Norse mythology, the magical artefacts of the gods – from weapons through jewels to steeds – often have names that bespeak the (at least desired) quality of the object. Thus, Odin's eight-legged horse is Sleipnir – "the Slipper" – a name suggesting its swiftness, while his magical self-reproducing ring is Draupnir – "the Dripper" – since it literally drips gold. Naming an object in this way seems to both bestow or intensify the desirable quality and most importantly to give the namer power over the artefact. We find similar fetishistic naming in other cultures and mythologies.

Tolkien, too, follows this practice: weapons, in particular, are given descriptive names. Elendil's sword Narsil means "red and white flame", referring to the darkness-vanquishing power of the sun and moon. At a less exalted level, in *The Hobbit* Bilbo gives his Elvish sword – in fact a dagger made in the First Age Elvish city of Gondolin – the name Sting, in the hope that it will enable him to wield it effectively against his enemies. The Three Rings, too, have names that encapsulate their elemental power: Narya, Nenya and Vilya respectively incorporate Quenya words for fire (*nár*), water (*nén*) and air (*vilya*). We might conjecture that the Seven and the Nine Rings also had names, although Tolkien does not reveal them (the Ring of Thror is not an exception since this is only an acquired nickname).

While possessing the name of an artefact or person connotes having power over that object or person, not naming, or refusing to name, something or someone suggests a reversal of that power dynamic – the object exerts power over the possessor or beholder. Among the ancient Israelites the name of god, YHWH, was so sacred, so fearful and so powerful that speaking it was forbidden; he was referred to only as Adonai, "lord". The trope of naming and not naming appears frequently in fantasy writing, perhaps most memorably in Ursula Le Guin's Earthsea novels and stories. In the island-world of Earthsea, being in possession of a person's or object's hidden name gives a certain power over them. Out of fear of their destructive power, the dreaded spirits of Atuan are called the Nameless Ones. We even find an echo of this trope in J. K. Rowling's Harry Potter sequence, where Lord Voldemort is superstitiously known as "He Who Must Not Be Named" or, more humorously, as "You-Know-Who".

Tolkien, too, seems to play on this theme. The Dwarves, for example, do not reveal their secret Dwarvish names to the outside world for fear of making themselves vulnerable, and we learn in *The Lord of the Rings* that Sauron does not allow his name to be either spoken or written by his followers, thus maximizing his power over them. We find the same logic in the naming of the Rings of Power: while the Elvish rings, entirely benign in their origin, are, as we have seen, named, the One Ring, whose sole function is to wield power over others, is nameless, too awful, too dreadful, to be named. Sauron, too, is the unnamed ruler of unnamed objects – the Lord of the Rings.

GUARD OF THE HOARD
MAURO MAZZARA

POWER, FAME AND DESTINY

The rings of Norse mythology – like Tolkien's – were commonly magical rings forged by elves. These gold rings were tokens of both power and eternal fame. They were also symbolic of the highest power: destiny, the cycle of doom. Indeed, the Domhring, the Ring of Doom – the ring of monolithic stones that stood before the Temple of Thor – was perhaps the most dreaded symbol of the violent law of the Vikings. (In Tolkien, an identically named "Ring of Doom" stands outside the gates of Valmar, the city of the Valar.) In the centre of this ring of stones was the thunder god's pillar, the Thorstein. The histories tell us of its use. In the ninth century the Irish king Cashel Maelgula Mac Dungail was made captive in the Viking enclave of Dublin. He was taken to the Ring of Doom and his back was broken upon the Thorstein. Of another such ring in Iceland a scribe in the twelfth century wrote that bloodstains could still be seen upon the central stone.

Among the Vikings, the gold ring was a form of currency, a gift of honour, and sometimes an heirloom of heroes and kings. (Such a ring belongs to the Swedish royal house, the Swedish kings' ring known as Svíagrís.) At other times, when great heroes or kings fell, and it was thought none other would be worthy of the honour of the ring lord, the ring-hoard was buried with its master.

So, in barrow and cave, in mere and grave, upon burial ship sunk beneath the sea, the rings slept with their ring lords. Afterward, tales were told of dead men's curses and supernatural guardians. In Norse myth and in Tolkien's tales, guardians of treasures and ring-hoards take many forms: damned spirits, serpents, dragons, giants, dwarves, barrow-wights and demon monsters.

DRAUPNIR

Tolkien's Rings of Power were explicitly finger-rings, but some of their cultural and mythological inspirations were undoubtedly arm-rings. Anglo-Saxon kings gave bonding gifts of silver, or more rarely gold, arm-rings – *béagas* – to their warriors, who wore them proudly not only as a sign of their prowess and loyalty but also as a token of their wealth and status. They were often exquisitely crafted, as evidenced by a rare surviving example found in Wendover, now in the British Museum. Arm-rings are quite frequently mentioned in *Beowulf*, a poem Tolkien was deeply familiar with, where the lord is referred to by the kenning *béag-gifa* – ring-giver.

Sauron, as the part creator and giver of the Nine Rings, can be perceived as a perverted version of the Anglo-Saxon lord. The Ringwraiths likewise are corrupted versions of the Anglo-Saxon warriors, using their gifts to accumulate wealth and prestige, but eventually succumbing entirely to Sauron's will and becoming slaves. The positive dynamic of king and warrior in Anglo-Saxon culture is inverted and parodied. One powerful inspiration for Tolkien's ring mythology – and especially of the One Ring – is the golden arm-ring Draupnir, "The Dripper", in Norse mythology. The ring belongs to the god Odin and was a gift from the dwarves. The chief attribute of the ring is that every ninth day it drips eight new rings – making nine rings in all. The ring's magic makes it a symbol of power and influence, specifically that between a king, or jarl, who gave arm-rings to his followers, often in recognition of success in battle. In Anglo-Saxon, a kenning for "king" was "ring-giver". Odin, as the ultimate king, is also thus "lord of the rings".

While Draupnir, in Norse mythology, in some sense represents social cohesion, hierarchy and mutuality, the One Ring is explicitly about power used solely to dominate. Sauron too is a ring-giver, but his motive in giving rings of power to Men and Dwarves is not to oil the wheels of Middle-earth society, but to disrupt it and remake it in his own image. While Odin is ultimately prepared to surrender Draupnir – in an act of humility he lays it on the funeral pyre of his son Baldr – Sauron will stop at nothing to repossess the One Ring. It is ultimately down to a humble Hobbit, Frodo Baggins, to attempt to abjure the power of the Ring in the fires of Orodruin (Mount Doom).

KING SOLOMON
MAURO MAZZARA

KING SOLOMON'S RING

The most famous ring legend in the Judeo–Christian tradition is the one linked with King Solomon. Tradition tells us that Solomon was not only considered a powerful king and wise man, but he was also believed to be the most powerful magician of his age. These magician's powers were attributed largely to his possession of a magic ring. The legend of "King Solomon's Ring" is certainly the one tale of the Judeo–Christian tradition that had the most profound influence on the imagination of Tolkien in his composition of *The Lord of the Rings*.

There can be little doubt that Tolkien was familiar with this ancient biblical tale of a sorcerer-king who (like Sauron) used a magic ring to command all the demons of the earth, and bent them to the purpose of ruling his empire. Just as Solomon uses his magic ring to build his great temple on Moriah, so Sauron uses the One Ring to build his great tower in Mordor. Of all rings of myth and legend, Solomon's Ring most resembles the One Ring of *The Lord of the Rings*.

Solomon's Ring is also like Sauron's One Ring in that its power can corrupt its master, even one as wise as Solomon. In the figure of the demon Asmodeus we see the subtle agent of evil who corrupts the wise but fatally proud King Solomon of Israel, and through possession of the ring causes his downfall. In the figure of the demon Sauron we see the subtle agent of evil who corrupts the wise but fatally proud King Ar-Pharazôn of Númenor, and through possession of the ring causes his downfall.

Curiously, the tale of Solomon's Ring also has elements that invite comparison with that other miraculous quest object of Tolkien's mythology. Just as the Elven King Thingol succeeds in acquiring the brilliant, light-radiating jewel called the Silmaril, so the Hebrew King Solomon succeeds in acquiring the brilliant, light-radiating jewel called the Shamir. Both are heirlooms of their races: the Silmaril was once the sacred jewel of the ancestral leader of the Elves, Fëanor; while the Shamir was the sacred jewel of the ancestral leader of the Jews, Moses. In Tolkien, the Silmaril is finally set into a gold headband and shines from the brow of the celestial traveller, Eärendil the Mariner, in the form of the Morning Star. Once the Shamir is returned to the Hebrews, the radiant jewel appears to fit perfectly on the golden bezel of Solomon's Ring. The jewel doubles the power of Solomon's Ring and illuminates the "One Name" of God.

MAGIC NUMBERS

In his elaboration of his ring legend, Tolkien must have been more or less conscious of the mystical and mythological associations of the numbers of rings, both in terms of the real world and within his own legendarium. While it is probably going too far to call such associations strictly numerological – as pertaining to the arcane art of number codes and patterning practised by writers, artists, architects . . . and charlatans, since ancient times – the writer clearly enjoyed playing with numbers and their symbolism. We see this in the Ring Verse itself, enumerating the twenty rings created by the Elves and Sauron in the Second Age, as recited by Gandalf to Frodo near the beginning of *The Lord of the Rings*.

NINE RINGS FOR MORTAL MEN
MAURO MAZZARA

CELEBRIMBOR AND THE FORGING OF THE RINGS OF POWER

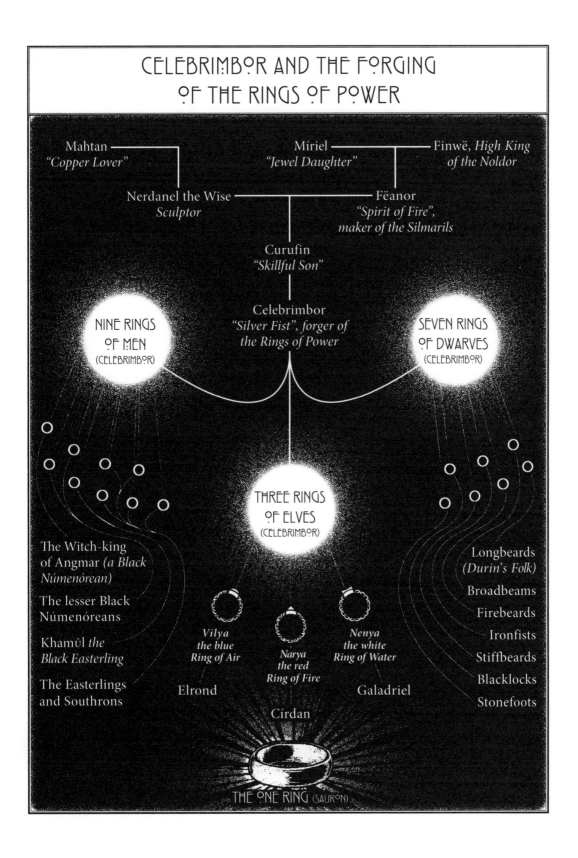

Mahtan "Copper Lover"

Míriel "Jewel Daughter"

Finwë, *High King of the Noldor*

Nerdanel the Wise *Sculptor*

Fëanor "Spirit of Fire", *maker of the Silmarils*

Curufin "Skillful Son"

Celebrimbor "Silver Fist", *forger of the Rings of Power*

NINE RINGS OF MEN (CELEBRIMBOR)

SEVEN RINGS OF DWARVES (CELEBRIMBOR)

THREE RINGS OF ELVES (CELEBRIMBOR)

The Witch-king of Angmar (*a Black Númenórean*)

The lesser Black Númenóreans

Khamûl *the Black Easterling*

The Easterlings and Southrons

Vilya the blue Ring of Air

Narya the red Ring of Fire

Nenya the white Ring of Water

Elrond

Cirdan

Galadriel

Longbeards (*Durin's Folk*)

Broadbeams

Firebeards

Ironfists

Stiffbeards

Blacklocks

Stonefoots

THE ONE RING (SAURON)

THE RINGS AND DEMOGRAPHICS

In the broadest terms, we might say that the number of rings correlates to the demographics of Middle-earth: "Mortal Men" are the most numerous of its peoples, populating numerous kingdoms across the continent, and are therefore given the most rings – nine. The Dwarves, we presume, are the next largest race – or at least have the next largest number of kingships, or houses – and thus possess seven rings. The Elves, by the Second Age, are the least numerous people of Middle-earth, with only a scattering of realms, and are thus associated with just three rings. There is just one Dark Lord, of course, and therefore just "One Ring to rule them all".

All these numbers – three, seven, nine and one – appear repeatedly across Tolkien's legendarium. Three, for example, seems to be a number closely associated with the Elves: there are three kindreds of Elves who make the journey to Valinor, and there are three Silmarils, the jewels forged by Fëanor that wreak such havoc during the First Age. Seven appears in the number of Palantír, or Seeing-stones, made in Númenor, and in the number of Fathers of the Dwarves. There are nine members of the Fellowship of the Ring (to correspond with the Nine Ringwraiths).

Beyond these internal recurrences of particular numbers, however, Tolkien also seems to be mining – and playing with – the real-world associations of numbers found in mythology and folklore.

NINE RINGS FOR MORTAL MEN

The number nine was especially significant in Norse mythology, where it had associations with magic and occult knowledge. The branches of Yggdrasil, for example, shelter nine worlds, the god Heimdall is the child of nine Wave Maidens, nine gods survive the apocalypse of Ragnarök … The number was especially associated with the god Odin, whom we have already seen as a prototype "Lord of the Rings", owner of the self-reproducing ring Draupnir, and possessor of deep, dark knowledge. Nine days and nights is the length of time Odin hangs on the gallows of the cosmic tree Yggdrasil so as to gain the secret knowledge of the runes.

Tolkien's Nine Rings of Men take up the relationship between the number nine and dark or forbidden knowledge. Some of the powerful Men who come to possess the Nine Rings begin as sorcerers and continue to practise dark magic through their careers, most notably the Witch-king of Angmar. The Nine Rings enable the bearers to prolong their life – the lust for immortality being one of the great "sins" of Men in Tolkien's ethos – but paradoxically bestows on them a living death, as wraiths, hovering between life and death just as Odin did as he hung from the branches of Yggdrasil.

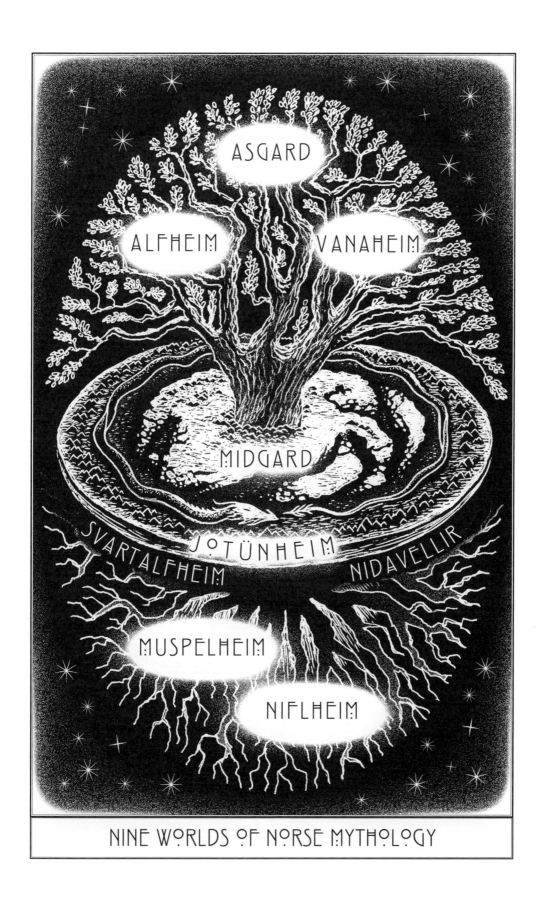

NINE WORLDS OF NORSE MYTHOLOGY

THE RINGS OF POWER IN THE SECOND AND THIRD AGES

1500 — 1500 *Rings of Power forged by Sauron and Elven-smiths of Eregion (Three Elf Rings, Seven Dwarf Rings, Nine Rings for Men*

1603 *War of Sauron and Elves. Three Elf Rings hidden (Gil-galad*   1600 *Sauron forges One Ring in Fires of*
in Lindon, Círdan in Grey Havens, Galadriel in Lothlórien)   *Mount Doom*

2000 —

2251 *Ringwraiths, slaves of the Nine Rings, come to serve Sauron*

2500 —

3000 —

3430 *Last Alliance of Elves and Men formed*
3441 *One Ring cut from Sauron's hand. Mordor falls. Sauron and Ringwraiths vanish*

SECOND AGE

1 *Gil-Galad's Elf-ring goes with Elrond to Rivendell*   2 *Battle of Gladden Fields. One Ring lost in*
Anduin River

500 —

1000 — 1000 *Sauron in Mirkwood, secretly gathers Rings*   1050 *Wizards come to Middle-earth. Círdan gives*
Elf-ring to Gandalf

1200 *Ringwraiths appear in north*

1300 *Lord of Ringwraiths becomes Witch-king of Angmar*

1500 —

1975 *Angmar destroyed*   1980 *Ringwraiths dwelling in Mordor*
2000 — 2002 *Witch-king begins rule in Minas Morgul*

2470 *Gollum takes One Ring into Misty Mountains*   2463 *One Ring found by Déagol in the Anduin*

2500 —

2845 *Sauron seizes last of the Seven Dwarf Rings*

2941 *Bilbo Baggins finds One Ring in the Misty Mountains*

3000 — 3018 *Fellowship of the Ring formed*   3001 *Bilbo Baggins gives One Ring to Frodo Baggins*

3021 *The War of the Ring begins. One Ring destroyed. Mordor falls.*
Sauron and Ringwraiths vanish forever

3021 *Keepers of the Elf Rings sail to Undying Lands*

THIRD AGE

SEVEN RINGS FOR THE DWARVES

One of the first of the prime numbers (after three and five) and thus heavily endowed with mystical symbolism, seven appears exhaustively in folklore and fairy tale: we all know that cats have seven lives and that the seventh sons of seventh sons have magical powers. The number also proliferates in the Bible – there are seven days of creation; seven pairs of each clean animal on Noah's Ark; Seven Seals in the Book of Revelation – as well as in classical antiquity – there were seven heroes who fought against the city of Thebes, seven hills of Rome, seven Wonders of the World, seven seas, seven "planets" (referring to "wandering" astronomical objects visible in the sky) ...

But why Seven Rings for the Dwarves? There are Seven Houses of Dwarves, as we've seen, and later there were Seven Hoards that grew on the foundation provided by each ring. It may be that Tolkien was merely using the number for its folkloric resonance – he may even have been thinking of the seven dwarves in the fairy tale of Snow White – but perhaps he was also thinking of the number's connotations of prosperity and wealth: seven is considered to be a lucky number worldwide and thus appropriate for the gold-, mithril- and jewel-loving race of the Dwarves.

Tolkien was often deeply inspired by the places he visited, and most especially by landscapes where the ancient past seemed very close to the surface. One such place, as argued by the Tolkien scholar Tom Shippey, was Lydney, Gloucestershire, where there were the remains of a Roman-British temple dedicated to the Celtic healing god Nodens on top of an Iron Age hillfort known as Dwarf's Hill. In the late 1920s, the site was re-excavated by the archaeologist couple Tessa and Mortimer Wheeler, who invited then relatively unknown Oxford scholar J. R. R. Tolkien to help them investigate the tablet inscriptions found at the temple. One of these was the curse relating to a ring: "To the god Nodens: Silvianus has lost his ring and given half (its value) to Nodens. Among those who are called Senicianus do not allow health until he brings it to the temple of Nodens. (This curse) comes into force again." Tolkien also wrote an appendix about Nodens for the Wheelers' archaeological report, relating him to the Irish hero Nuada Airgetlám, Nuada of the Silver-Hand.

As several scholars have pointed out, there is a cluster of motifs here that can be related to Tolkien's own ring legend: a cursed ring, dwarves (and therefore smithery) and a god/hero known as Silver-Hand, the meaning of the name Celebrimbor. Whether consciously or not, Tolkien's poetic imagination may have absorbed these disparate strands and reformulated them in his story of Eregion.

THREE RINGS FOR THE ELVES

The number three is a sacred number in many cultures around the world and thus perfectly accords with Tolkien's Elves, the most "spiritual" of the peoples of Middle-earth. Deities, especially female ones, have often been worshipped in triads since ancient times, perhaps reflecting the three phases of the moon (new, waxing and full) – in Greek mythology, for example, we find three Fates, three Graeae (Grey Sisters) and originally three (rather than nine) Muses. In the early twentieth century – at the time Tolkien was writing – there was much theorizing about a supposed ancient Triple Goddess who had once been pervasive across Indo-European religion (see Robert Graves's *The White Goddess*, 1948). The triadic nature of the divine – though in male form – can also be found in Christianity, in the Holy Trinity of God the Father, Jesus Christ and the Holy Ghost. For some commentators, the eventual bearers of the Three Rings – Gandalf, Galadriel and Elrond – are a mythologized representation of the Trinity, as saviours of Middle-earth in the Third Age.

Once again, though, it is Norse numerology that seems to have most deeply influenced Tolkien's choice of Three Elven Rings. Norse deities often possessed magical artefacts in threes: Odin, for example, has the ring Draupnir, the spear Gungnir and the eight-legged horse Sleipnir; while Freyr has the ship Skidbladnir, the boar Gullinbursti ("Golden Bristles"), as well as a sword that fights by itself. Moreover, perhaps more suggestively we find both elf- and dwarf-smiths making trios of artefacts as gifts for the gods: in the *Prose Edda* the Sons of Ivaldi – who appear to be elves – make the aforementioned Skidbladnir and Gungnir together with a replacement head of golden hair for the goddess Sif, while the dwarves, in rivalry, make Gullinbursti, Draupnir and Thor's Hammer, Mjolnir.

NINETEEN

We cannot entirely discount there might be other, more obscure number associations.
Aside from the One Ring, there are nineteen rings altogether for the peoples of Middle-earth. Nineteen is another prime number and has a number of arcane associations, perhaps the most notable of which is the nineteen-year Metonic cycle, or enneadecaeteris – a calendrical period recognized by many ancient cultures that measures the time it takes for the moon's phases to recur at the same time of the year. Make of this what you will. The Rings of Power have associations with nature and the elements, so perhaps the lunar connection is not so far-fetched.

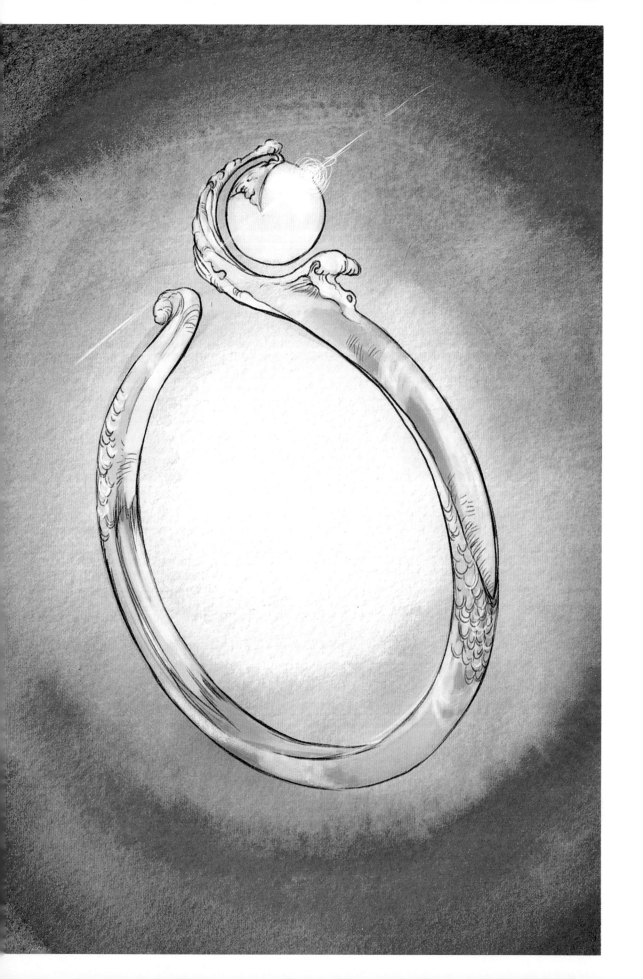

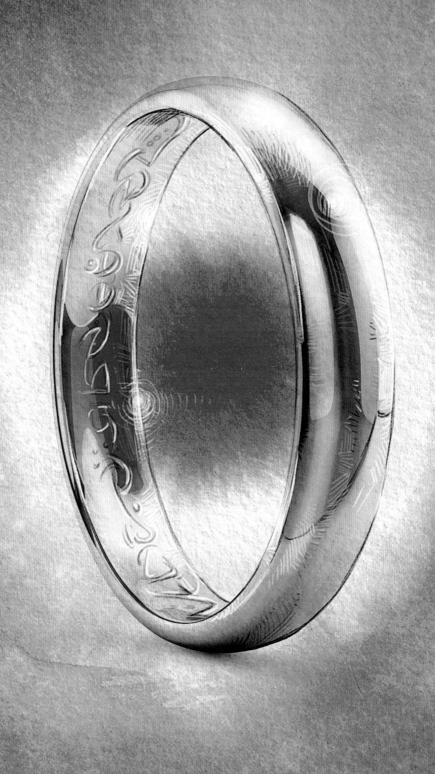

THE ONE RING
MAURO MAZZARA

THE ONE RING – GOOD AND BAD ALCHEMY

We shouldn't forget the number one in our discussion of ring numbers. In the Neoplatonist philosophy of Plotinus and Philo, "The One" is the ultimate reality, the source of all creation, just as one is the source of all other numbers; it is the godhead. Tolkien seems to be referring to this in his name for his primordial creator spirit, Eru, whose name means simply "The One" in Quenya.

The One Ring appears to both echo and subvert this meaning. The "Ring Verse" describes how the One Ring is created to transcend the multifariousness of the other rings, binding them together, and ruling over them. The intention of the forger of the One Ring, Sauron – the Dark Lord who stands in opposition to Eru – is to bind the other rings in darkness, not in light: his ultimate goal is to bring unity to the world, but under his dominion – a parody and inversion of the mission of Eru, out of whose oneness grows the multifariousness of creation.

Gandalf's Elf ring and Sauron's One Ring are both symbolic of the control of alchemical fire, but alchemical fire of different types. The evil alchemy that made the One Ring commands the dark satanic fire out of the bowels of the earth. This power transforms the material world – or at least gives that illusion – and the accompanying illusion of world power. The good alchemy of Gandalf's Elf ring commands the celestial fire of the spirit. This "good" alchemical fire has no power over the material world. However, the fire of the spirit does have the power to impassion and uplift the soul because ultimately its source is the sacred "Flame Imperishable" of Eru the One – the Supreme Being who gave all things life.

This head-on conflict, of course, leads to mutual destruction. Gandalf foresees this, but makes the sacrifice because no other way is possible. However, Gandalf also understands that ultimately the only way to defeat Sauron and his evil One Ring is not to attempt to overthrow him or to seize its power, but to undo the alchemical process by which the Ring of Power has been made. Once Gandalf understands the "language of the ring", he knows that only by reversing the alchemical process can Sauron be defeated. Just as common folklore tells us one can undo a spell by reciting it backward, so Gandalf understood that the only way the One Ring could be destroyed was to reverse the process by which it was made. This was the reason for *The Lord of the Rings*' "backward" ring quest. The One Ring had to be taken back to the crucible where it was made. Only there in the fiery furnace of the "Cracks of Doom" where it was forged could the One Ring be unmade – and Sauron's power destroyed.

In its creation, Sauron's One Ring was the ultimate heresy against the alchemical tradition. It was the evil opposite of the Ouroboros, or serpent ring of the alchemist. When Sauron came to the Elven-smiths of Middle-earth and persuaded them to forge the other Rings of Power, he came in disguise as Annatar, "giver of gifts". He appeared as a benevolent alchemist very like the Greek hero Prometheus. In fact, he was the exact opposite. Prometheus's ring marked the saviour who enslaved himself and gave mortals freedom, knowledge and life. Sauron's ring marked the tyrant who enslaved the world and gave mortals bondage, ignorance and death.

RINGS IN ALCHEMY: A SECRET LANGUAGE

The ring was also the symbol of the alchemist. The alchemist's ring – in the form of a serpent swallowing its own tail – represented a quest for knowledge that was forbidden by the Church. Alchemists were often executed as sorcerers or magicians. The practices of these alchemists were often linked with their rings. The real or imagined use and trade of such "rings of power" were perceived as an evil that must be eradicated.

Because of constant persecution, alchemists cloaked their studies in secrecy and wrote up their experiments and formulae in codified records. The twentieth century's leading historian of religions, Mircea Eliade, concluded that alchemical studies were transmitted mystically, just as poetry uses fables and parables. Regarding alchemy, Eliade wrote: "What we are dealing with here is a secret language such as we meet among shamans and secret societies and among the mystics of the traditional religions."

This "secret language" is strongly reminiscent of the "magic speech" of the ring referred to in the Exeter Book, a tenth-century compendium of Anglo-Saxon poems. It seems likely that we are dealing with the same kind of cryptic communication. The "magic speech" of the ring and the "secret language" of alchemy are one. The dominance of the symbol of the ring in pagan religions – and in all shamanistic tribal cultures that use metal – is related to the ring's alchemical origins.

The symbol for the alchemist was a gold ring in the form of a serpent swallowing its own tail. This serpent ring is the Ouroboros, meaning a "a tail biter", a symbol for eternity that is found in a score of mythologies. In many cultures we find in the great serpent the first form to emerge from chaos; it then encircles the void and creates time and space by forming a ring, becoming the Ouroboros and grasping its own tail. We see this celestial serpent ring in the Babylonian serpent called Ea, the Greek Ophion, the Hindu Shesha, the Chinese Nāga and the Norse Jörmungandr.

The ring was a symbol of the alchemist's profession and a vision of the alchemist's quest. This was a ring very like that seen in a vision by the seventeenth-century metaphysical poet Henry Vaughan, in his poem "The World". To the alchemist, the ring shaped like, or engraved with, the "eternal" serpent and made of "immortal" gold was the symbol for universal knowledge. It was – one might say – the "One Ring" by which all others are ruled. The power of the alchemist traditionally evolved through a combination of natural science and supernatural wisdom, which are embodied in the crafts of the shaman and the smith. These are derived from the symbols and mysteries of metallurgy, and are ultimately emblematic of the physical and spiritual mastery of fire.

Traditionally, the alchemist – like the magician and the smith – is given the title "master of fire". The smith's mastery of fire is obvious enough in his forging of metals. The magician – from the most obscure tribal shaman to Tolkienian Wizards like Gandalf – handles fire and flame as a demonstration of mastery of spiritual power. Indeed, in many cultures the magicians, fakirs and shamans are traditionally renowned for walking on hot coals and spitting fire. The alchemist employs both physical and spiritual fire to transform the natural world.

In Tolkien's world of *The Lord of the Rings*, we have the ultimate evil alchemist in the form of Sauron, the Ring Lord. Sauron is both a magician (or sorcerer) and a smith who forges the supernatural One Ring of Power. He has the perfect evil alchemist's pedigree. He was originally a good fire spirit apprenticed to the Vala Aulë the Smith. He betrayed his master and became the disciple of Melkor, the Dark Sorcerer. Through a combination of his skills as a sorcerer and a smith, he creates the ultimate weapon in his One Ring of Power. We are told that the mortal Easterlings and Southrons saw Sauron as both king and god and feared him, for he surrounded his abode with fire. Sauron built the Dark Tower of Mordor near the fiery volcano of Mount Doom.

THE SERPENT
JOHN DAVIS

THE SORCERER
IAN MILLER

ALCHEMY AND SORCERY

Many races fall quickly and easily under the spell of the One Ring, but those enemies of Sauron who cannot be immediately enslaved are resilient chiefly because they too possess elements of alchemical power. These are the Noldor Elves, the Dwarves and the Númenóreans.

The greatest of these are the Noldor Elves, who are already gifted with "Elven magic" before they become the students and disciples of Aulë the Smith. (In Tolkien's original drafts the Noldor were actually called the Gnomes, from the Greek *genomos*, meaning "earth-dweller"; while *noldor* is Elvish for "knowledge", just as Gnostic – the alchemical sect – is from the Greek *gnosis*, meaning "knowledge".) Greatest of the Noldor Elves is Fëanor (meaning "spirit of fire"), who in *The Silmarillion* combines Elvish spells and a smith's skills to forge the famous Silmarils. These are the "jewels of light" stolen by Sauron's master, Melkor, the Lord of Darkness, and over which the wars of the First Age are fought. Fëanor's grandson is the Noldor prince Celebrimbor, the Lord of the Elven-smiths of Eregion, who forges the Rings of Power, over which the wars of the Second and Third Ages are fought.

The Dwarves are also tough opponents who possess elements of alchemical power, for they are a race who were shaped by Aulë the Smith. They are resilient to fire both physical and sorcerous. They are a stubborn race who mark their weapons and armour with Dwarven runes and spells. The greatest of the Dwarves was Telchar the Smith, whose weapons are blessed with such powers that one (the knife called Angrist) is used to cut a Silmaril from Melkor's (Morgoth's) iron crown; and another (the sword Narsil) is used to cut the One Ring from Sauron's hand.

The Númenóreans and their Dúnedain descendants on Middle-earth learn their alchemical skills from the Noldar Elves and the Dwarves, and in some creations even outdo their masters. So, as the Dúnedain of the North and the Men of Gondor are the surviving descendants of these great people, and the chief inheritors of ancient wisdom which gives them the power to resist evil temptation, these people are seen by Sauron as the chief obstacles to his domination of Middle-earth. However, there are also the Istari, or Wizards, who have been sent by the Valar to Middle-earth as adversaries of Sauron the Ring Lord. Yet, of the five Wizards who came, only Gandalf is able to stand against Sauron. For it is Gandalf wearing Narya – the Elf "ring of fire" – who best understands the alchemical nature of the conflict with Sauron. It is Gandalf who discovers and translates the "secret language" of the One Ring which is "written in fire".

THE WAR OF THE ELVES AND SAURON

Although the War of the Elves and Sauron marks a crucial turning point in the history of the Second Age, it is easy to forget its importance given the cataclysmic events that overwhelm Middle-earth at the very end of the age. It is also something of a misnomer since not only the Elves but also the Dwarves of Khazad-dûm and the Númenóreans play a crucial role in the ultimate defeat of Sauron: the war is in fact a powerful prefiguration of the War of the Last Alliance, showing what can be achieved when Elves, Men and here also the Dwarves work together.

As a boy, Tolkien was perhaps typical of his peers in liking the grand sweeping movements and engagements of armies across landscapes – at least as told in the histories of ancient times (he was far less fond of the realities of war, experienced on the ground, as in his service as an officer during the First World War). Something of this excitement comes across even in his brief account of the War of the Elves and Sauron: lightning attacks, rear assaults, sieges and pincer movements are all involved.

The war is the end of the beginning and the beginning of the end. It is the moment when Sauron finally shows his hand after his duplicitous dealings with the Elves during the forging of the Rings of Power. And his ultimate defeat and retreat to Mordor, leaving swathes of Eriador wasted, will lead him ultimately to essay a more vulnerable flank of the Alliance – Númenor. The stage is set for the double denouement of the Second Age: the fall of Númenor and the War of the Last Alliance.

SOLDIERS

IAN MILLER

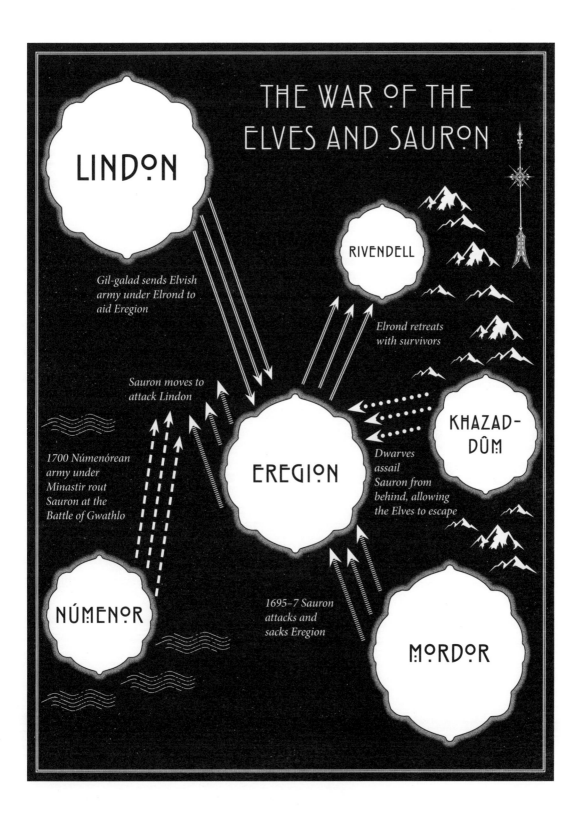

THE WAR OF THE ELVES AND SAURON

LINDON

RIVENDELL

Gil-galad sends Elvish army under Elrond to aid Eregion

Elrond retreats with survivors

Sauron moves to attack Lindon

KHAZAD-DÛM

1700 Númenórean army under Minastir rout Sauron at the Battle of Gwathlo

EREGION

Dwarves assail Sauron from behind, allowing the Elves to escape

NÚMENOR

1695–7 Sauron attacks and sacks Eregion

MORDOR

PART THREE

THE DOWNFALL OF NÚMENOR

FROM c. 2221 Kings of Númenor begin to question the Ban of the Valar: opposing factions of the King's Men and the Faithful emerge

3117 Númenóreans forbid the Elves from visiting Númenor and ban the use of Elvish languages

3175 Repentance of Tar-Palantir

3177 Civil war breaks out in Númenor between the King's Men and the Faithful

3209 Birth of Isildur

3219 Birth of Anárion

3255 Tar-Palantir dies, and Ar-Pharazôn seizes the Sceptre

3261 Ar-Pharazôn lands at Umbar

3262 Ar-Pharazôn takes Sauron prisoner

3310 The Great Armament begins

3319 Downfall of Númenor and the Changing of the World; Sauron flees back to Middle-earth

3320 Foundation of the Realms in Exile – Arnor and Gondor

3429 Sauron takes Minas Ithil

3430 Númenóreans in exile and Elves form Last Alliance

3431 Last Alliance marches to Imladris

3434 Battle of Dagorlad; Siege of Barad-dûr

3441 Deaths of Gil-galad and Elendil; defeat of Sauron; Isildur takes the One Ring of the Realms in Exile – Arnor and Gondor

WAVE OVER NÚMENOR
KIP RASMUSSEN

INTRODUCTION

The Downfall of Númenor is the dramatic highpoint of Tolkien's narrative of the Second Age. The primary source – which he freely admitted – was the ancient Greek story of Atlantis. But, clustering about his tale is a wealth of other influences – from the biblical story of the Flood, through real-world catastrophes, to a host of folklore about drowned lands. As readers, too, we are likely to view the Downfall through our own cultural lens, whether that pertains to local folklore, recent floods in our country or region, or a general anxiety about the climate crisis and rising sea levels. In the current climate, where Pacific and Indian Ocean islands are threatened with permanent inundation, we are all likely to empathize with Tolkien's (and Faramir's) recurring "Atlantean" dream of a great wave sweeping over a green, wooded island.

The major source for the Downfall of Númenor is the *Akallabêth*, which appears as the fourth part of *The Silmarillion*, edited by Tolkien's son and literary executor Christopher, and published posthumously in 1977. Thirty pages in length, it is the longest sustained narrative of the Second Age. There is an abbreviated account of the Downfall in Appendix B of *The Lord of the Rings*. Tolkien, however, had been working on versions of the story since the late 1930s; the original version was eventually published in the fifth volume of *The History of Middle-earth* (1987).

THE FAITHFUL AND THE KING'S MEN

In his narrative of the Downfall of Númenor, Tolkien is careful to provide a deep-rooted, somewhat complex history that underpins the island-kingdom's ultimate demise. The drowning of the island arises out of a slow, though seemingly inevitable decline as the people lose sight of the old ways and grow greedy for wealth and dominion. Tolkien's history centres around a factional divide that first emerges during the reign of the fourteenth king, Tar-Ancalimon (reigned 2221–2386 SA): between, on the one hand, the King's Men, who might, in modern terms, be described as nationalists – resistant to the Elves and their languages and culture, and militant about Númenor's right to wealth and power – and, on the other, the Faithful, who remain loyal to the old ideals, to the Elves and, ultimately, to the Valar. Tolkien complicates matters by showing how the King's Men are supported by the vast majority of the Númenórean population, the ordinary folk, while the Faithful are essentially a cosmopolitan elite led (at first in secret) by the Lords of Andúnië. Over time, the factionalism deepens, until under Ar-Pharazôn the hostility breaks out into outright barbarism, as the king sacrifices members of the Faithful in the Temple.

While Tolkien largely portrays the Númenórean factions in somewhat black-and-white terms, this conflict cannot fail but remind us of any number of deep-seated factional conflicts in human history – from the Blues and Greens of the sixth-century Byzantine Empire to the Whigs and Tories of late seventeenth- through mid-nineteenth-century Britain to the deep nationalists and democratic liberals entrenched in Western states today. Tolkien is always clear about who, in Númenor, is on the right side of history: very few real-world historical factions, after all, end up as demon-worshipping oppressors who practise wholesale human sacrifice.

NÚMENÓREAN KING

VICTOR AMBRUS

DECADENCE

Towards the end of the nineteenth century and into the twentieth, the notion that the West was in a period of decline or decadence preoccupied many intellectuals, especially those on the political right. The most influential among these was German philosopher of history Oswald Sprengler (1880–1936), who in his two-volume study *Decline of the West* (1918 and 1922) contended that all civilizations, like natural organisms, went through a cycle of birth, flourishing, decline and death, and that Western civilization was already in decline, would be in its death throes by the time of the new millennium, and would eventually collapse. In many ways, Sprengler's ideas echoed those of early Christian thinkers like St Augustine of Hippo (354–430 CE), who likewise saw the Roman Empire as in a process of terminal moral and material decline.

One of the most celebrated paintings of the nineteenth century was *Romans in Their Decadence* (1847) by Thomas Couture (1815–79), a massive canvas showing an orgy of drinking and lovemaking under the censorious eyes of antique statues. The accompanying salon exhibition catalogue made the moral of the painting clear by quoting two lines from the Roman satirist Juvenal (c. 55–? CE): "Crueller than war, vice fell upon Rome and avenged the conquered world." Tolkien portrays the late Númenóreans as revelling in much the same decadent spirit, spending their time – while not subjugating the Men of Middle-earth – in feasting and carousing and developing a taste for fine clothes and jewels.

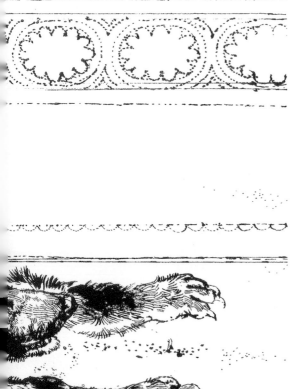

TOLKIEN'S DREAM: LITERARY THERAPY

In his letters, Tolkien speaks repeatedly of his recurring dream of a green, wooded island overwhelmed by a Great Wave. Tolkien clearly saw this in psychological, Jungian terms since he called this dream recurrence his "Atlantis complex" – according to the Swiss psychologist Carl Jung (1875–1961), a complex was a structure of the psyche that brings together and crystallizes thoughts, feelings and memories. Tolkien also spoke of the dream as having been inherited and that he had passed it on to his second son, Michael Tolkien (1920–84), so he seems to have thought of it too as a kind of "race memory". In Jungian terms, we might argue that the drowning of Atlantis is an archetype of the universal unconscious passed down through the generations, connecting the almost buried memory of an ancient catastrophe with more current fears – war, nuclear annihilation, societal breakdown and so forth. In *The Lord of the Rings*, Tolkien gives his dream to Faramir, a descendant of the Númenórean Faithful, whose recurring dreams of the downfall of Númenor relate to the growing threat of Sauron and the storm clouds of war rising over the mountains of Mordor.

In his letters, Tolkien also reveals how the writing of the *Akallabêth* – which took place primarily in the 1940s – finally seems to have released him from his dream of catastrophe. By reimagining the drowning of an ancient island-kingdom, in an act of literary therapy he was finally able to exorcise the "Atlantis-haunting".

THE DEATH OF AR-PHARAZÔN
MAURO MAZZARA

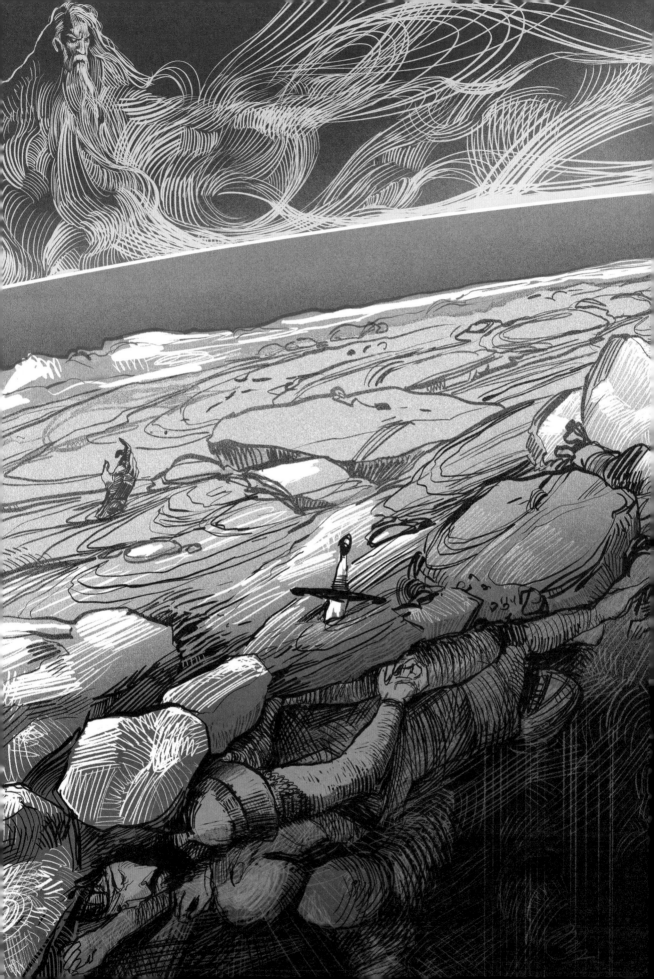

THE BAY OF NÚMENOR
KIP RASMUSSEN

PLATO'S ACCOUNT

We mostly remember Plato's Atlantis for the story of its downfall, but Plato himself was far more interested in its government and politics (an interest that Tolkien himself shared in his depiction of Númenor) and treated its demise only cursorily in the closely related dialogues *Timaeus* and *Critias* (both c. 360 BCE). There, the Athenian oligarch Critias (or some other statesman with the same name) gives an account of how, nine thousand years before, the Atlanteans had come to subjugate the peoples of North Africa and western Europe and eventually came into conflict with the Athenians, who against all odds were able to overthrow the empire. Soon after, Atlantis – seemingly as a punishment for its hubris and impiety – as well as parts of western Europe and Africa as well – was destroyed in a cataclysm of earthquakes and floods:

> "But afterwards there occurred violent earthquakes and floods; and in a single day and night of misfortune all your [i.e. Athenian] warlike men in a body sank into the earth, and the island of Atlantis in like manner disappeared in the depths of the sea. For which reason the sea in those parts is impassable and impenetrable, because there is a shoal of mud in the way; and this was caused by the subsidence of the island."
>
> – *Timaeus*, trans. Benjamin Jowett

Tolkien seems to take up several elements of Plato's story: the imperial hubris of the Númenóreans is implicated in their downfall; not only do the evildoers die, but also the good; and the island, of course, is destroyed in a great sea flood that also alters the coastline of Middle-earth. Tolkien largely removes the earthquakes from the final Númenórean cataclysm but implies them instead in his account of the destruction of Ar-Pharazôn and his men when they set foot in Aman and are buried beneath a great rockfall or landslide.

DROWNED LANDS

The folkloric motif of the drowned land or city is found in many regions around the world. In part, such tales may catch dim, fragmentary memories of past cataclysms, but they also represent a poetic truth – the awareness that all things pass: human lives, cities and civilizations. Stories of surviving mountaintops piercing through the waves – as in Tolkien's lost Númenor – or church bells heard tolling underwater during calms are haunting reminders of the transitoriness of existence and human endeavour.

While Atlantis – the Western prototype of the drowned land – was Tolkien's primary inspiration for Númenor, he would have also been aware of the many similar tales that clustered around Europe's western fringes. Like Númenor, too, such tales often had a moralistic slant – the cataclysm these lands meet comes about because of the impiety or immorality of the inhabitants, with only a select few managing to escape, by the grace of the gods. Accounts were no doubt influenced by the fate of the cities of Sodom and Gomorrah in the book of Genesis, where a people are destroyed (by earthquake and fire in this instance) and only a chosen few escape (Lot and his family).

THE LOST LANDS OF LADROS
PETER PRICE

←———————≪

YS, CANTRE'R GWAELOD AND OTHER CELTIC LOST LANDS

The cluster of folkloric tales of drowned lands on Europe's Celtic fringes is perhaps a recollection of the precariousness of life and landscapes at the very edges of what was then (to Europeans) the known world. In Brittany, there is the tale of the rich port city of Ys, or Kêr-Is, in the Bay of Douarnenez, whose existence was ensured by the building of a strong dyke. The king's wicked daughter, however, secretly opened the dyke gate one night to let in her lover and the ocean swept in, drowning all the inhabitants, who were in any case not much better than the princess. With the help of a saint, only the good king escaped, galloping away from the city on horseback. As usual, we may note similarities and differences between the fate of Ys and Númenor – in Tolkien we find a doubling of roles: the sinful king, Ar-Pharazôn, is destroyed and it is the good king-to-be, Elendil, who, by a miracle, is saved.

Similar tales reverberate around the British Isles and mutually influenced one another. In Wales, we appear to have no fewer than three lost lands – Maes Gwyddno (later called Cantre'r Gwaelod) in what is now Cardigan Bay, often billed as the "Welsh Atlantis"; the Realm of Teithi Hen off St David's in Pembrokeshire; and Tyno Helig, in Conway Bay in North Wales, to the east of Anglesey. In most of the tales the drowning likewise is caused by neglect or impiety. In Maes Gwyddn, a young woman allows a well to overflow, and in its alter-ego, Cantre'r Gwaelod, a man gets drunk and forgets to shut the floodgate. Small sins, we might think, for such a punishment. In Tolkien, by contrast, almost the entire people – though grossly misled by just one, Ar-Pharazôn – has gone astray and fallen into evil.

BEYOND THE MOUNTAINS
ŠÁRKA ŠKORPÍKOVÁ

LYONESSE

Accounts of the lost land of Lyonesse between the western tip of Cornwall and the Scilly Isles may have come about because of a literary mistake. Lyonesse is most famous as the home of the Arthurian knight Tristan, and medieval French adaptors of the Matter of Britain rather hazily conceived of "Léonois" – in fact the region of Lothian in Scotland (in Latin Lodonesia) – as lying adjacent to Cornwall. Once the French romances were adapted back into English – for example in Sir Thomas Malory's *Le Morte d'Arthur* (1485), Lyonesse took on a life of its own, although it continued to be rather shadowy.

The drowning of Lyonesse is non-Arthurian, emerging in post-medieval times, perhaps to explain the evident lack of such a place in British geography. The story goes that the inhabitants committed a crime against God so heinous that he destroyed them overnight, sending a great wave that submerged the country and drowned every one of its inhabitants, save a lucky few. Alfred, Lord Tennyson (1809–92) acknowledges such tales in the "The Passing of Arthur" section of his *Idylls of the King* (1859–85), a poetic cycle the Victorian-born Tolkien would have been familiar with. There the poet describes Lyonesse as:

> A land of old upheaven from the abyss
> By fire, to sink into the abyss again;
> Where fragments of forgotten peoples dwelt,
> And the long mountains ended in a coast
> Of ever-shifting sand, and far away
> The phantom circle of a moaning sea.

The story of a lost land and a lost king (Arthur) may easily have fed into the young Tolkien's imagination.

Coincidentally, recently underwater archaeologists have conjectured that the Isles of Scilly may have once formed several bigger islands and that there may be the remains of settlements off the present coastline.

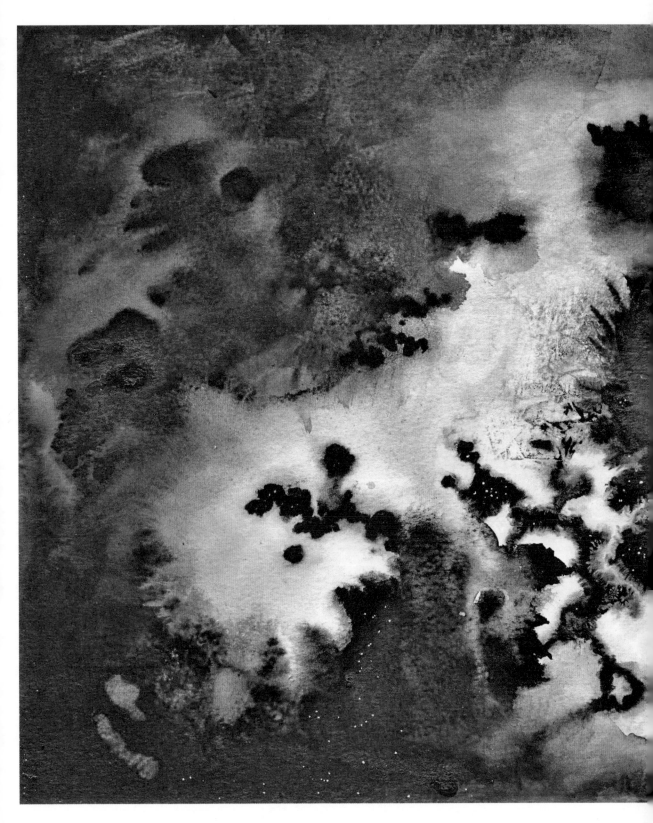

BELEGAER — THE GREAT SEA

In the Third Age – the age of *The Hobbit* and *The Lord of the Rings* – the great crucible around which the narratives revolve is the Misty Mountains, the massive backbone of Middle-earth that sweeps hundreds of leagues southwards down through its western reaches. Crossing the mountains, whether over or under, provides the decisive moment in both narratives – shifting the protagonists into an ever more dangerous world.

For much of the Second Age, by contrast, it is the Great Sea, Belegaer, that acts as the crucible. For one thing, with the drowning of Beleriand, the sea has become much, much bigger, and, with the rise and fall of the island Númenor at its heart, this becomes an age of daring sea voyages, coastal exploration and colonization, and, towards its end, naval adventurism. Only in the latter half of the age does the focus begin to swing to the Misty Mountains, with the forging of the Rings of Power in Eregion, deep in their shadow. After the Downfall and the Remaking of the World, the Great Sea increasingly becomes a peripheral, dangerous, and almost mystical space – broached only by departing Elves and marauding Corsairs.

The centrality of the sea in the Second Age may remind us of the role of the Mediterranean in the Bronze Age and classical worlds, crisscrossed by trade routes and dotted with busy ports. We may be tempted, too – especially given the siting of Atlantis beyond the Pillars of Hercules – to draw an analogy between the Belegaer and the Atlantic – especially during the Age of Exploration, as European navigators set sail into the west and "discovered" new worlds where new possibilities and new societies seemed in the offing. Númenor, too, appears, at first, as one such "brave new world", although in the end it fails to live up to its utopian promise.

ULMO HOLDS BACK THE GREAT SEA
KIP RASMUSSEN

NOAH'S FLOOD, AND SODOM AND GOMORRAH

Flood narratives are present in many mythologies of the eastern Mediterranean and Near East. Most anciently, there is a flood myth in the Babylonian *Epic of Gilgamesh* (written c. 2100–1200 BCE) – preserved in the so-called Tablet XI (the "flood tablet") discovered in Nineveh. In it, the gods plan a flood (we assume to rid the earth of a decadent humankind) but command one man, Utnapishtim, to build a boat and to load onto it individuals of all the animals, as well as his relatives and craftsmen, so that humanity can start afresh. The tale is replicated in Greek mythology in the story of Deucalion and Pyrrha, and, of course, most famously in Noah's Flood, in the book of Genesis, in which the patriarch Noah takes much the same role as Utnapishtim and through his sons is responsible for repeopling the Earth.

Noah's Flood, in particular, seems to have been present in Tolkien's mind as he developed his story of the Downfall of Númenor. In a 1951 letter, he called Elendil – the last lord of Andúnië and leader of the Faithful who foresightedly prepares a fleet of nine ships in his homeland and thereby manages to escape the catastrophe – "a Noachian figure". Elendil and his sons Isildur and Anárion, like the patriarch Noah and his sons Seth, Ham and Japheth (we should never expect full correspondences), will go on to renew civilization – both physically and morally.

Another biblical parallel for the Downfall is the story of the destruction of Sodom and Gomorrah, also told in Genesis. Just as with antediluvian humanity, God punishes the "cities on the plain" because of their sinfulness, though not until he has met Abraham's bargain that he mete out punishment only if the patriarch fails to find ten good people in Sodom. The city fails the test, and God rains down fire on both Sodom and Gomorrah. Only Abraham's nephew, Lot, and his family survive, led out of Sodom by angels, and even Lot's wife dies when, disregarding the angels' warning, she turns to look at the burning city and is turned into a pillar of salt.

Here we find elements that are common to many accounts of the downfalls of cities and civilizations, including Tolkien's own account of Númenor: a sinful, unrepentant people; a swift, terrible and wholesale retribution, and a handful of good survivors, miraculously saved. The fate of Lot's wife may seem cruel – her crime apparently curiosity or nostalgia or just plain disobedience – and so likewise the death of Míriel on the drowned slopes of Meneltarma appears a harsh punishment of an innocent.

GILGAMESH
IAN MILLER

──────

AR-PHARAZÔN – GILGAMESH AND PHARAOH

While Ar-Pharazôn – the twenty-fifth and last king of Númenor – is the great villain of the *Akallabêth* narrative, Tolkien is careful to imbue him with all the flawed grandeur of a tragic hero. His story – from his seizing of the throne from his cousin and rightful heir, Tar-Míriel, through his seduction by Sauron to his terrifying fall that brings cataclysm to his land and people – may bring to mind all manner of Shakespearean characters, from Macbeth (who likewise seizes the throne and brings chaos to the kingdom of Scotland) to Coriolanus, another great military figure who is corrupted by his pride.

Ar-Pharazôn is depicted not as inherently evil but as a mighty soldier who conquers vast territories in Middle-earth and sets himself against Sauron (though, admittedly, because he is a threat to his own power rather than the embodiment of evil). The king's name means "Golden" in Adûnaic – suggesting both his sun-like greatness and his inevitable fall that follows the seeming zenith of his power, when he defeats Sauron in Middle-earth and brings him back to Númenor in chains. Ar-Pharazôn falls, like many of the tragic heroes before him, because of his vaulting ambition and pride. Bought up under the influence of the King's Men, his mind is already warped. In many ways, he is the last great flowering of the Númenórian spirit but also encapsulates the flaws that were inherent in Tolkien's conception of this people from the start. His rise and fall recapitulates the whole history of this island-nation.

Perhaps Ar-Pharazôn's – and the Númenóreans' – greatest flaw is the fear of old age and desire for immortality, which is what finally drives the king to rebel against the Valar and set sail to seize the Undying Lands. This lust to live forever invites comparisons with the Babylonian hero Gilgamesh, "two thirds divine and one third mortal", in the Babylonian epic that bears his name, who, after the death of his friend Enkidu, becomes afraid of death and sets out to distant lands to try and win immortality, a gift of the gods. Unlike Ar-Pharazôn – who remains vainglorious to the moment of his destruction – Gilgamesh finally realizes the futility of his quest and returns to his homeland, defeated and despondent, but alive.

KINGS AND SUNS

Kingship has been associated with the sun since ancient times – kings were glorious rulers who surveyed and gave life to the world over which they held sway. The Egyptian pharaohs, for example, saw Amun-Ra, the sun god and king of the gods, as their patron. In honour of Amun-Ra, Amenhotep III (reigned 1391–1353 BCE) took the epithet "the dazzling sun", while his son, Akhenaten (1353–1336 BCE), made the sun god, now named Aten, the sole deity of the Egyptian pantheon.

The king–sun association survived into early modern times and the rise of the European absolute monarch, who stood at the centre of his kingdom, just as the sun was now known to stand at the centre of the solar system, in the Copernican model of the universe. Most famously, Louis XIV (reigned 1643–1715), another expansionist and ambitious king, called himself the Sun King and developed a state cult, visible in the paintings and sculptures in the Palace Versailles and its gardens, that depicted him as Apollo, the far-shining Greek and Roman sun god.

Ar-Pharazôn the Golden, likewise, sets himself up as a sun king, embarking, like Louis, on a massive programme of military campaigns, undertaking a building programme that might have vied with that of Versailles, and wielding the power of life and death over his people.

THE TEMPLE TO MELKOR
PETER PRICE

THE TEMPLE

Tolkien was a devout and observant Catholic and during his long years in Oxford attended Mass almost on a daily basis. He admitted that *The Lord of the Rings* was "a fundamentally religious and Catholic work", although his beliefs pervade the work at the level of myth – of sin, resurrection and redemption – rather than as explicit ideas. Neither Eru the One – clearly a stand-in for the Christian God – nor the angelic Powers of Arda, however, are worshipped, but are only revered, by Elves, Men and Dwarves. There is certainly no organized religion in Middle-earth: we do not find churches in the Shire, temples in the cities of the Elves, or sanctuaries in the delvings of the Dwarves, and there are certainly no priests or monks, though we might argue that the Wizards, especially Gandalf and Radagast, have an air of wandering friars about them. The individual's relationship with the Powers appears to be communicated, above all, through a closeness to nature – for example the trees of Yavanna, the stars of Varda or the silver, gold, mithril and jewels of Aulë – and expressed, in person or communally, through supplication, prayer and song.

In this context, Ar-Pharazôn's foundation of the Temple in Númenor's capital, Armenelos, seems shocking, flying in the face of all the legendarium's "rules": it is devoted to the worship of Melkor/Morgoth (the original Dark Power), Sauron serves as its high priest, and human sacrifice is regularly practised. While the Temple may have its origins in the temple of Poseidon that Plato mentions in his account of Atlantis, its Númenórean equivalent appears to be a sacrilegious inversion or perversion of a Catholic church, perhaps even of St Peter's Basilica in Rome (both are crowned with massive domes). The human sacrifice of slaves may seem to parody the transubstantiation that takes place during the Roman Catholic rite of the Eucharist – the bread and wine becoming the flesh and blood of Christ, who sacrificed himself freely on the cross. The Aztec practice of human sacrifice and cannibalism (the latter not mentioned by Tolkien as one of the sins of the Númenóreans, though we can well imagine it) was certainly sometimes viewed in this way by the Catholic priests who accompanied the conquistadors.

THE ULTIMATE SIN

One of the most disturbing details in the downfall of Númenor is the human sacrifice that takes place in the Temple, built by Al-Pharazôn under the influence of Sauron. The victims of the sacrifice are most often the Faithful, who are killed in the hope that Morgoth – the object of the cult – will grant the Númenóreans immortality, something which of course is outside his ability to gift.

This gory detail will perhaps bring to mind the human sacrifice practised in many ancient civilizations, the Aztecs for example, but especially the child sacrifices of the people of Carthage – a Phoenician colony that flourished from around 800 BCE until 146 BCE. The practise was widely reported on by ancient Greek and Roman writers (as well as early Christian ones), and was for a time thought of by modern scholars as Roman propaganda against this important and powerful enemy of the Roman state. In more recent times, the Carthaginian practise of human sacrifice as portrayed in even more lurid terms – Gustave Flaubert's sensationalist novel *Salammbô* (1862), set in ancient Carthage, included a chapter devoted to the sacrifice of children to Moloch, a Canaanite god whose name may remind us of Tolkien's fallen angel Melkor (who later became the Dark Lord Morgoth). In recent years, archaeological investigations have shown that child sacrifices did in fact take place in the city and on quite a large scale.

In Tolkien's narrative, as in Flaubert's *Salammbô*, the introduction of human sacrifice is meant to suggest the depths of depravity to which a once-great civilization has fallen. After this greatest of crimes, there is really no way back: Númenor must fall.

THE SHADOW AND ORIGINAL SIN

Tolkien frequently uses the term "The Shadow" in his writings about Middle-earth, often as a euphemism for the Dark Lords, Morgoth and Sauron, for the Ringwraiths, or for their empire over the peoples of Middle-earth, but also as a euphemism for a more general falling away into corruption and even evil, from which no people, it seems, are spared. In terms of Tolkien's history of Númenor, it is used repeatedly to describe signs that the Númenóreans are turning away from the Valar, and that they are beginning to hanker after those things that are forbidden them or outside their gift, notably the immortality of the Elves and the right to step upon Aman itself (the Ban of the Valar), causing the marring of the original "bliss" of the island-kingdom. There are clear parallels here, of course, with the Christian doctrine of the Fall and Original Sin, as outlined especially by St Augustine of Hippo (345–430 CE). Inside the heart of every human lies an inescapable taint – inherited sin consequent upon the disobedience of Adam and Eve in the Garden of Eden (Genesis 3). The Númenóreans, originally living in a state of Edenic bliss, eventually and ineluctably fall into sinful disobedience – culminating in the ultimate sin of Ar-Pharazôn's assault on Aman.

THE SHADOW
PETER PRICE

BIRDS OF ILL-OMEN

Omens abound in European mythology and medieval literature, reflecting times when aberrations in the natural order were interpreted as signs of divine displeasure or impending doom and punishment. The harbingers of doom were very often birds: in ancient Greek, the word for "bird", *ornis*, also meant "omen", and soothsayers called oionomanteis (bird interpreters) carefully read the ornithological world for messages from the gods. Ravens, crows and screech owls were considered as especially unfavourable signs. The interpretation of birds as omens survived into early modern times: in Shakespeare's play *Macbeth*, an old man relates how "On Tuesday last, / A falcon, towering in her pride of place, / was by a mousing own hawk'd and kill'd" (II.iv.11–13), an unnatural event interpreted as presaging the murder of good King Duncan.

Tolkien seems to refer to this superstition in his account of the Downfall, where Manwë sends huge storm clouds in the shape of eagles as a warning to the Númenóreans. The chief of the Valar was especially associated with the Great Eagles, who serve as his emissaries and eyes, so the clouds were a potent reminder of the respect owed to the divine order and of the power of divine retribution.

◄———◄

THE GREAT ARMAMENT

Tolkien gives us very few clues as to what Númenórean ships looked like, though what he does reveal shows that they were very different indeed from the graceful swan-ships of the Elves, who initially taught the Men of Númenor the craft of shipbuilding. The Elves used their boats primarily for travelling, up rivers and across the sea, and with their elegant lines, single sails and prominent prows in the shape of swan necks and heads – as depicted in Tolkien's fiction as well as in his artworks – they were clearly akin to Viking long-ships, though without the latter's function as weapons of war and conquest.

Over 3,000 years, Númenórean ships undoubtedly changed, both technologically and aesthetically, transforming as their primary function altered from exploration – during the days of the peaceful mariners Vëantur and Aldarion – to empire-building. By the time of the Great Armament, they had probably evolved into something like the war galleons of the Renaissance period – multi-masted, massive, threatening, as seen in Ar-Pharazôn's mighty black-and-gold flagship, the *Alcarondas* – meaning "Castle of the Sea", although Tolkien may also have had in mind the latest iron-clad, steam-powered ships of the Victorian Royal Navy, likewise intended to "rule the waves". The flagship's name has a certain Spanish ring to it, bringing to mind also the Great Armada of 1588, when 130 Spanish ships set sail to conquer England.

Under the influence of Sauron, and as part of his plan to become the dominant power in not only Middle-earth but also Aman, Ar-Pharazôn begins a rapid expansion and upgrade of the Númenórean navy known as the Great Armament. Tolkien was doubtless aware that this was also the popular name given to the expansion of the British Royal Navy in the mid-nineteenth century, in the wake of the Crimean War against Russia in 1854–6. The power of Britain's navy lay not only in its size but in its technological innovation: by 1856, Queen Victoria's fleet comprised 247 steam-driven ships, out of the 254 total. This helped cement Britain's place as a world superpower and played a key role in the maintenance of British imperial rule in the late nineteenth century.

Ar-Pharazôn built his new navy in the western ports of Númenor, so his intentions against Aman and the Valar were clear. Likewise, Britain's ships were largely built in the great imperial shipyards of its western reaches: in Glasgow, Liverpool and Belfast. The year 1860 saw the launch of the HMS *Warrior*, the first armour-plated, iron-hulled steam-powered warship, although she was quickly surpassed in power by the mast-less HMS *Devastation*. Tolkien may have had such terrifying ships (and others that followed) in mind when he conceived of Ar-Pharazôn's flagship, *Alcarondas*, the "Castle of the Sea", with its impressive black and gold sails.

However we imagine the ships in detail, their evolution charts the imperial rise and simultaneous moral fall of the once-great Númenórean nation.

THE GREAT ARMAMENT
MAURO MAZZARA

THE CAVE OF THE FORGOTTEN

As soon as Ar-Pharazôn sets foot on Aman, he and his men are buried by the hills of Calacirya – the Cleft of Light that leads into Valinor, home of the Valar. The bodies of the king and his army are buried in the so-called Caves of the Forgotten, only to be released to fight at the time of the Last Battle at the end of time. The image of a king and his followers imprisoned in a cave brings to mind King Arthur and his knights who are said to sleep in a cave, waiting to be summoned in Britain's hour of need. Similar tales were told of many kings, even purely historical ones, such as Charlemagne and Fredrick Barbarossa, and there are many fairy tales dealing with a king who sleeps under a mountain whom passers-by disturb at their peril.

It is not clear what role Ar-Pharazôn and his men are to play in the Last Battle – whether they were to fight on the side of the Valar or Morgoth, of good or evil – although perhaps Tolkien imagined the moment to be redemptive, much as he showed the redemption of the Oathbreakers (the Dead Men of Dunharrow) in *The Lord of the Rings*.

THE ARMY OF THE DEAD
IAN MILLER

THE CHANGING OF THE WORLD

Tolkien's Arda – the Earth – undergoes numerous re-shapings through its long history. It is, however, the Downfall of Númenor that causes the most extraordinary geophysiological change in the fabric of Arda. When Ar-Pharazôn sets foot in Aman, the Valar relinquish their authority over it and call on Eru to intervene. The One creates a massive rift in Arda between Númenor and Aman, and the world, having previously been flat, bends round to meet itself to form the near-spherical planet we know today. Aman, in the meantime, leaves the fabric of Arda altogether, now reachable by only the Straight Road – a mystical sea voyage that can be taken only with the permission of the Valar, as is granted to the Elves and others (including Frodo and Bilbo at the end of *The Lord of the Rings*).

We may be tempted to relate Tolkien's rather baffling concept to the shift from the flat Earth model to the spherical Earth model that took place first in sixth-century BCE Greece (although it did not become widely accepted in Greek thought until two centuries later or more). Later in life, Tolkien himself seems to have abandoned the idea that Arda was ever flat. The removal of Aman from Arda, meanwhile, turns that continent into a paradisical otherworld, attainable only by the blessed.

THE STRAIGHT ROAD
MAURO MAZZARA

ELENDIL — SUPER-PATRIARCH

Elendil – the last lord of Andúnië – and his two sons, Isildur and Anárion, are pivotal figures in Tolkien's unfolding history of Middle-earth – transitional figures who bridge the "old kingdom" of Númenor with the "new kingdoms" of Gondor and Arnor, and, in the case of Isildur, the Second and Third Ages. The legendarium's historiography is essentially cyclical: this triad of Tolkienian heroes in some ways reproduces the triad of Eärendil–Elros–Elrond who provide the bridge between the First and Second Ages.

Elendil begins, as Tolkien noted, as a "Noachian figure" who, foreseeing disaster, builds a fleet of nine ships for the Faithful and escapes the Downfall of Númenor by a miraculous wave that brings him to Lindon – the kingdom of Gil-galad – and his sons to the Bay of Belfalas, hundreds of miles to the south. To take up Tolkien's own biblical analogy, however, he is also a Mosaic figure, who on bringing his people to a new "promised land" proclaims in Quenya: "Et Eärello Endorenna utúlien. Sinomë maruvan ar Hildinyar tenn' Ambar-metta" – "Out of the Great Sea to Middle-earth I am come. In this place will I abide, and my heirs, unto the ending of the world." And in his struggle against Sauron and as a military commander, he finally becomes analogous to a third biblical patriarch – Joshua – the warrior who after Abraham's death leads his people to victory over the people of Canaan, overthrows the walls of Jericho, and establishes the tribes of Israel. In the single figure of Elendil, then, Tolkien creates a kind of super-patriarch – saviour, leader and warrior.

THE HILL-MEN
MAURO MAZZARA

TERRA NULLIUS?

From a contemporary perspective in particular, the setting up of the two Númenórean kingdoms over swathes of western Middle-earth may give us pause for thought. Elendil's arrival in Lindon and his cry claiming possession over the land for himself and his heirs may recall European explorers landing on unknown shores and laying claim to the lands of the Americas or Australia, on the grounds that they were somehow "empty", "virgin" lands only waiting to be settled and ruled over – a concept known in Latin as *terra nullius* – no one's land. And yet we know that, before the arrival of the Dúnedain – the Men of the West – Middle-earth already had large populations of Men, just as there were numerous indigenous Americans or Australians, and with their own civilizations that may have been less sophisticated technologically than, but of equal validity to, the civilization of Númenor.

Elendil's declaration may seem doubly and even triply arrogant in that he has just landed in Elvish territory – Lindon is the kingdom of Gil-galad – and he has come from a kingdom that has already shown itself to be morally bankrupt. Whether Tolkien was aware of such ironies is a matter of debate. In all likelihood he perceived the arrival of the Faithful and the new kingdoms in a much more positive light than we are able to muster with our postcolonial hindsight – as the creation of settled rule where once there had been a state of anarchy and a potential bulwark against Mordor, should that "state" ever rise again.

DUNLENDING
IAN MILLER

THE TWO KINGDOMS

There are many feasible real-world historical analogies for the South-kingdom and North-kingdoms of Gondor and Arnor, although as always such analogies should not be applied rigorously or pedantically. Tolkien's Middle-earth was above all born out of one individual's creativity and imagination, not as a systematic conglomeration of influences and correlates. Attempts to calque the history of Europe (or wherever) directly onto the history of Middle-earth are intriguing but ultimately fruitless and even detrimental to our appreciation of the author's extraordinary imaginative feats. Nonetheless, given Tolkien's education – at Birmingham's longstanding King Edward's Grammar School, and subsequently at the University of Oxford, where we would have been steeped in both the classics and the Bible – we can surmise that both these sources helped shape his two great kingdoms of Middle-earth.

One possible model, then, was the twin Israelite kingdoms of Israel and Judah, which historically seem to have come into being in the ninth century BCE; the Bible tells us that previously the states had existed as a united monarchy under Kings Saul, David and Solomon. There are some pleasing parallels here with Tolkien's Númenórean kingdoms-in-exile, which likewise lie adjacent to one another, north and south, and which also existed for a time as a unified kingdom. While we have already noted other biblical resonances, further than that we dare not, and perhaps should not, go: Osgiliath as Jerusalem, Annúminas as Samaria? Such one-to-one correspondences quickly become reductive.

Another possible influence frequently cited is the Roman Empire, especially during its decline and breakup into western and eastern parts, although here the analogies work best in the Third Age, when both internal and external pressures cause the Realms-in-Exile to contract, fragment and, in the case of Arnor, collapse altogether. From this perspective – if we turn our conceptual map ninety degrees counterclockwise – Arnor might be viewed as the Western Empire, with its capital, Annúminas, as Rome, and Gondor as the long-surviving Eastern (or Byzantine) Empire, with Osgiliath or Minas Tirith as Constantinople. In the end, again, such comparisons break down quite quickly, become tiresome and fail to throw any light on the wonder of Tolkien's creation. Perhaps as far as possible we should try to engage with Tolkien's world on its own terms, appreciating the influences that may have shaped them but not allowing them too much ground.

ANNÚMINAS
founded
3320
by Elendil

Arnor

ELOSTIRION
founded after
3320
by Elendil

AMON SÛL
founded after
3320
by Elendil

ORTHANC
likely founded
between
3320 and 3340
by the
Dúnedain

Gondor

Mordor

MINAS
ANOR
founded
3320
by
the Faithful

OSGILIATH
founded
c. 3319
by
Isildur and
Anarion

MINAS
ITHIL
founded
c. 3320
by
the Faithful

BARAD-
DÛR
founded
1000
by Sauron

KINGDOMS AND FORTRESSES
OF THE SECOND AGE

THE GATES OF ARGONATH
KIP RASMUSSEN

SHARED KINGSHIP

Although Isildur is the elder of the two sons of Elendil, and Númenor used primogeniture when determining who inherits the throne, Isildur and Anárion share the kingship of Gondor, a testament perhaps to their friendship. Such shared rule is found mythographically in the twins Romulus and Remus, the founders of Rome, although here the foundation of the new city coincides with an act of fratricide when the brothers are unable to agree upon on which hill to build – the Aventine or the Palatine? – and Romulus, in some versions, ends up killing his brother. Isildur and Anárion appear harmonious, although we might detect an echo of the Roman dispute in the fact that the brothers rule from different citadels – Isildur out of Minas Ithil on the eastern side of the River Anduin and Anárion from Minas Anor on the river's western side; Tolkien's royal brothers' ability to compromise, however, is seen in their shared foundation of Gondor's capital, Osgiliath, on the River Anduin itself, with its great stone bridge seeming to symbolize their unity and equality.

Another pair of mythological brother-kings, Amphion and Zethus, joint rulers of the Greek city-state of Thebes, might represent a better model of harmonious diarchy (double kingship). Here the brothers bring complementary skills to their rule, seen in their building of the city's great walls: while Zethus is a warrior and offers brawn, setting stone upon stone using sheer slog, Amphion is a musician-magician, conjuring the stones by dint of the music of his lyre. We get no sense of this complementary rule in Isildur and Anárion, whose kingship is symmetrical as the twin cities they build either side of the Great River. The brothers are essentially mirror images of each other, although, narratively speaking, Anárion remains a much more shadowy figure than his elder sibling.

DIARCHY

Tolkien may also have been thinking of the diarchy practised historically in many ancient civilizations, where it helped to ensure the stability of the state. Sparta is perhaps the most famous example of ancient diarchy, although in this case the co-ruling kings came from two different dynasties, not one. Tolkien complicates the situation even further, since the Númenórean territories of Middle-earth are in fact ruled by a triarchy, or triumvirate: with the brothers' father, Elendil, acting as high king over both Arnor (his own kingdom) as well as Gondor. Again, triumvirates were quite common historically, most famously in the late Roman Republic, although there the setup was roundly unsuccessful: the so-called First Triumvirate (60–53 BCE) of Gaius Julius Caesar, Gnaeus Pompeius Magnus and Marcus Licinius Crassus was for all three a matter of expedience and ambition rather than a desire to serve the state. In the Third Age, Elendil and his sons will be viewed as near-legendary ideals, even if Isildur is eventually to fall victim to the power of the One Ring.

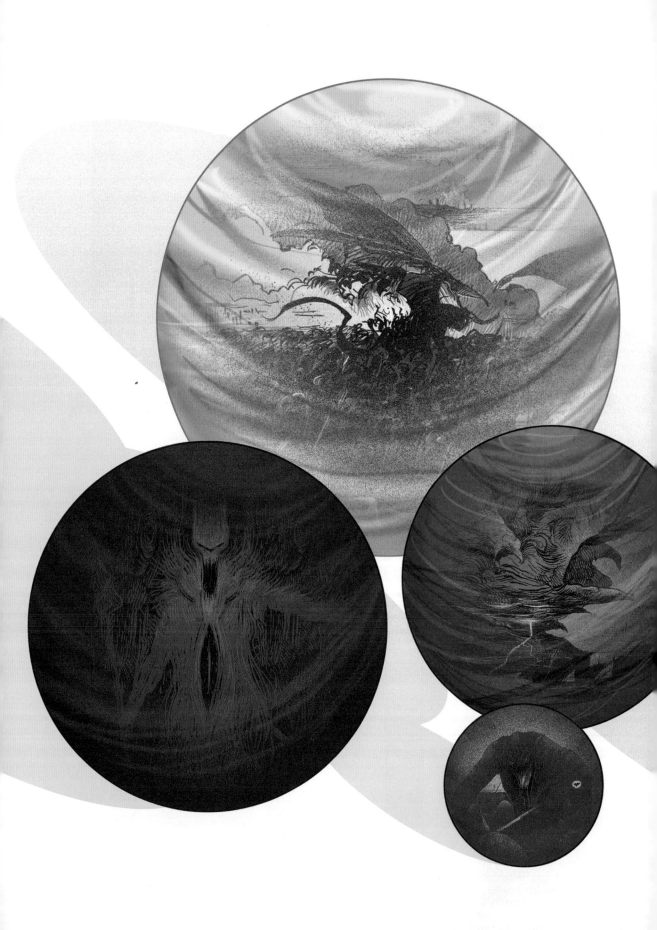

THE PALANTÍRI

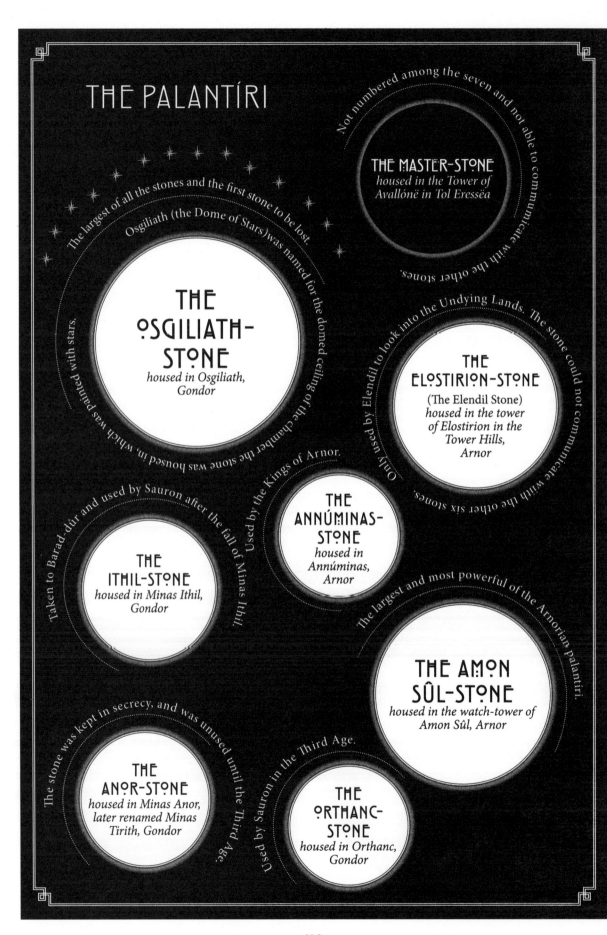

Not numbered among the seven and not able to communicate with the other stones.

THE MASTER-STONE
housed in the Tower of Avallónë in Tol Eressëa

The largest of all the stones and the first stone to be lost.

Osgiliath (the Dome of Stars) was named for the domed ceiling of the chamber the stone was housed in, which was painted with stars.

THE OSGILIATH-STONE
housed in Osgiliath, Gondor

Only used by Elendil to look into the Undying Lands. The stone could not communicate with the other six stones.

THE ELOSTIRION-STONE
(The Elendil Stone) *housed in the tower of Elostirion in the Tower Hills, Arnor*

Used by the Kings of Arnor.

THE ANNÚMINAS-STONE
housed in Annúminas, Arnor

Taken to Barad-dûr and used by Sauron after the fall of Minas Ithil.

THE ITHIL-STONE
housed in Minas Ithil, Gondor

The largest and most powerful of the Arnorian palantíri.

THE AMON SÛL-STONE
housed in the watch-tower of Amon Sûl, Arnor

The stone was kept in secrecy, and was unused until the Third Age.

THE ANOR-STONE
housed in Minas Anor, later renamed Minas Tirith, Gondor

Used by Sauron in the Third Age.

THE ORTHANC-STONE
housed in Orthanc, Gondor

THE PALANTÍRI
MAURO MAZZARA

THE PALANTÍRI — COMMUNICATION, EMPIRE, PROPAGANDA

The Faithful are not the sole survivors of the Downfall; artefacts and heirlooms – symbols both of how much has been lost and what might be regained – also make their way back to Middle-earth on the nine ships of Elendil. They provide a material link that connects and transcends lands and ages. *The Lord of the Rings*, set at the end of the Third Age, brims with glamorous Númenórean objects – from swords and trees to more magical artefacts – adding appreciably to the story in terms of intriguing narrative depth. In his writings about the Second Age, meanwhile, Tolkien provided the rich heritage of these objects.

Tolkien provides an especially deep history for the palantíri – "seeing stones" first made by the Noldor (and possibly by the arch-Elven-smith Fëanor) in Valinor even before the beginning of the First Age. They are dark, smooth spheres of varying sizes – presumably made out of some crystal-like rock (Tolkien may have been thinking of obsidian, see below) – that enable communication between users over hundreds, if not thousands, of leagues. Users could also not only share thoughts but also see unfolding events, as permitted by the other user. Successful use of the palantíri depended on the skill and power of the user, as poor Peregrin Took discovers to his cost when the comes across the stone kept by Saruman at Orthanc.

Scrying – the use of artefacts such as mirrors, bowls of water and crystal balls as methods of clairvoyance or divination – has been practised by cultures since ancient times, used to see the past, present and future, and sometimes to communicate with the dead. In Persian mythology, the Cup of Jamshid – which in some stories takes the form of a globe – was said to reflect back the whole world to the viewer; on its wise use a king's empire was said to depend – a description that seems to parallel the use of the palantíri for the good governance of the Númenórean Realms-in-Exile. The famous court astrologer and magician John Dee (1527–1608), advisor to Elizabeth I of England, made use of a scrying stone (seerstone) made from obsidian (so, like the palantíri, black), and proposed the creation of a philosopher's stone that would somehow magically enable the English queen to set up a European empire.

The Eldar gifted a number of the palantíri to the Faithful, who brought them to Middle-earth and set them up in towers across their new kingdoms, at strategically key locations, as a communications network (it is almost as if they and Tolkien envisioned the mobile communications networks of the modern age).

As with the Cup of Jamshid and Dee's philosopher's stone, the palantíri were key to the smooth running of the Númenórean kingdoms, allowing the Dúnedain to communicate over great distances; in the Third Age, the loss of various of the palantíri and the breakdown of the communications system they support appears to be closely entwined with the breakdown in the Númenórean Realms-in-Exile.

The palantíri are among the most intriguing objects in *The Lord of the Rings*, in that, used by various parties to communicate, spy and deceive, they appear to have parallels with real-world wartime media phenomena and technologies. Both Saruman and Denethor attempt to use the palantíri to spy on and control the enemy but thereby become entangled in Sauron's "media manipulation"; only Aragorn proves powerful and wise enough to turn the tables on Sauron and use the Orthanc stone to manipulate him into bringing forward his attack on Gondor and thus overlook the Ring-bearer's trek into Mordor.

THE SCEPTRE OF ANNÚMINAS

The Sceptre of Annúminas is another Númenórean artefact that makes an appearance in *The Lord of the Rings*, brought by Elrond, in whose safekeeping it has long been, to Minas Tirith, to give to King Elessar, as the new king of the Reunited Kingdom of Gondor and Arnor. In the days of Númenor, this silver sceptre, modelled on a similar sceptre carried by the kings of Númenor, was in the possession of the Lords of Andúnië and thus came to Middle-earth in the possession of Elendil, borne by him as high king and by all subsequent kings of Arnor. Given Númenor's Egyptian influences, Tolkien may have been thinking of the *was*, a staff carried as a sign of authority by the pharaoh and appearing in many carvings and wall paintings in the hands of men as well as gods. Sceptres, however, were also carried by the kings of Mesopotamia and Judah, by the ancient Greeks and Romans, and by many other subsequent kings and queens. Symbolically, the sceptre stands in for the weapon once wielded by the ruler to assert his dominion and as such is a metaphor for state violence transferred and deferred.

THE SCEPTRE OF ANNÚMINAS
JAMIE WHYTE

THE RING OF BARAHIR
JAMIE WHYTE

THE RING OF BARAHIR

Of all the heirlooms brought to Middle-earth, the Ring of Barahir is among the most venerable, made, like the palantíri, by the Noldor in Valinor before the beginning of the First Age. While entirely "unmagical", the ring was a potent symbol of the friendship of Elves and Men. Initially gifted by the Elven king Finrod Felagund to the Edain Barahir as a sign of their friendship after Barahir rescues the king from almost certain death during the Dagor Bragollach (Battle of the Sudden Flame), it is passed down through the generations in the face of calamity until it enters the possession of Elros, first king of Númenor, who bequeaths it to his eldest child and daughter Silmariën – down whose line, through the Lord of Andúnië, it descends to Elendil.

The ring is one of the rare artefacts in Tolkien's legendarium that remains unsullied or uncorrupted: it is given freely and is not the object of lust or covetousness and therefore becomes a symbol of hope in the face of calamity. This seems to be the meaning behind the ring's insignia (the badge of Finarfin's house) – twin serpents meeting at a crown of flowers, one upholding the crown, the other devouring it; a yin-yang–like symbol of ultimate harmony in the flux of fortune and misfortune. It is only apposite that, in *The Lord of the Rings*, Elendil's heir, Aragorn, gifts the ring to Arwen, the grand-niece of Finrod. The circle is complete.

NIMLOTH AND THE WHITE TREE
JAMIE WHYTE

LAURELIN AND TELPERION
PAULINE MARTIN

➵——→

TREES — A MORAL BAROMETER

Trees play a major role in Tolkien's legendarium, providing not only awe-inspiring backdrop to the narrative but also serving as potent symbols and even as actual characters, from the amoral Huorns of the Old Forest to the kindly Ents of Fangorn. Forests loom large in almost every region – as homelands for the Green Elves but also as a lair for more murderous creatures, such as the super-sized Spiders of Mirkwood. That said, a place entirely without trees is an evil place indeed – Mordor is a treeless, smoking plain. Númenor is an island rich in trees of many kinds, and its downfall is heralded by its rulers' willingness to cut down vast forests in Middle-earth to build its navy.

For Tolkien, then, trees had a moral resonance – for him, the ability to care for nature is a sign of a healthy relationship not only with Earth/Arda but also with divinity. The most resonant of the Valar for Tolkien is perhaps Yavanna, the maker of all living things who at the very beginning of Arda sings into being the Two Trees of Valinor, the silver Telperion and the golden Laurelin. From Telperion is descended the tree of Nimloth that stood in the King's Court in Númenor's capital, Armenelos, and once again the success or failure of its preservation serves as a moral barometer of the Númenórean people and their king. Its eventual burning by Sauron in the Temple to Melkor signals the island-nation's moral collapse, while its rebirth as the White Tree of Minas Ithil is the promise of a Númenórean resurrection in Middle-earth.

FOURTH
WHITE TREE
planted by Elessar
Minas Tirith

THIRD
WHITE TREE
planted by Tarondor
Minas Tirith

SECOND
WHITE TREE
planted by Isildur
Minas Anor

FIRST
WHITE TREE
planted by Isildur
Minas Ithil

NIMLOTH
Númenor

CELEBORN
Tol Eressëa

GALATHILION
created by Yavanna
Túna

TELPERION
created by Yavanna
Valinor

THE DESCENT OF NIMLOTH

THE WHITE TREE — NIMLOTH

Like the Palantíri, the White Tree of Númenor is bound up with kingship, empire and continuity, but is also a symbol of piety. The tree was a gift to the Númenórean kings from the Elves of Tol Eressëa and was a sapling of their sacred tree Celeborn, itself a sapling of Galathilion in Valinor, grown by Yavanna from a seedling of, or possibly in imitation of, the tree Telperion. This last was the silvery "moon-tree" that, with the "sun-tree" Laurelin, provide light to Middle-earth in some of its earliest days, before their destruction by Morgoth and Ungoliant. During Númenor's long history Nimloth grew in the King's Court – which we might imagine as an open terrace visible to all – before the King's Palace in Armenelos.

Because of its deep connections with the Elves and the Valar and the sacred time of Arda's earliest history, the Númenóreans' neglect of Nimloth is a measurement of their decline and impiety. The destruction of the tree in the Temple, at the hands of Sauron, re-enacts the destruction of Telperion by Morgoth and is thus the near-ultimate act of impiety (with the landing on Aman as the ultimate). Before its destruction, Isildur manages to gain access to the King's Courtyard – now a forbidden place – and steal one of its fruits – an act that has all kinds of mythological precedents such as Heracles' pilfering of the Apples of the Hesperides as well as fairy-tale ones such as the Grimm brothers' "The Golden Bird" where the thief of the king's prized fruit is the titular, phoenix-like bird. The fruits in such tales have associations with immortality and resurrection – and thus resonate with Isildur's theft, an act of pious criminality that ensures the continuity of Númenórean tradition (we might even conceive of his act as a reversal of Eve's theft of the fruit in the Garden of Eden).

Isildur takes Nimloth's seedling to Middle-earth where he plants it at Minas Ithil, as a symbol of the rebirth of Númenor and its true, original values in Middle-earth. The White Tree of Gondor is later used as the insignia of the kingdom, a tree emblem that may recall the Royal Oak as the symbol of the United Kingdom, commemorating the Shropshire oak tree in which the future Charles II took refuge after the Battle of Worcester (1651). The present Royal Oak, like the White Tree, is a seedling of the original tree.

NARSIL

We can conjecture that Elendil and his people brought many weapons with them to Middle-earth, some of which they already prized as heirlooms from the First Age. Of these, Narsil was undoubtedly the most venerated: originally made by the Dwarf Telchar of Nogrost in the First Age, it eventually came into the possession of the Lords of Andúnië. The sword plays a key role in the history of Middle-earth – wielded by Elendil during the War of the Last Alliance, broken at the Siege of Barad-dûr, and the shards eventually reforged at Rivendell as Aragorn's sword Andúril.

The association of swords and kingship is, of course, a long one. From the Bronze Age until medieval times, swords were "cutting-edge" military technology, majestic instruments of power and terror. In the story of Theseus, the hero only discovers his identity as the rightful heir to the throne of Athens when, nearing manhood, he lifts a boulder and discovers his father's sword and sandals beneath. Swords, stones and kingship similarly come together in the revelation of Arthur as the "once and future king" of Britain after he pulls a magical sword out of a stone.

SIGMUND AND GRAMR
MAURO MAZZARA

GRAMR — A SWORD REFORGED

Tolkien's primary inspiration for Narsil, however, comes from the Norse *Volsungsaga*. There Odin appears at a royal wedding and thrusts the sword Gramr ("wrath") into a tree that grows in the middle of the feast hall, announcing that whoever can draw the sword "will receive it from me as a gift and he will find out for himself that he never bore in hand a better sword than this". Only the bride's brother, Sigmund, can rise to the challenge, and uses it to become a mighty warrior, although it is eventually broken by Odin during Sigurd's final battle with his arch-enemy, King Lyngvi. Sigmund's wife, Hjördis, gathers up the shards as an heirloom for her as yet unborn son, and the sword is eventually reforged by the dwarf-smith Regin, to be used by Sigurd to revenge his father by killing Lyngvi.

Tolkien reformulates these elements for his sword Narsil, expanding its forging and reforging over thousands of years and generations, but retaining the essential story of rebirth and justice: Aragorn will be instrumental in destroying Sauron, who long ago killed his ancestor, Elendil.

SAURON'S DECEIT OF AR-PHARAZÔN
KIP RASMUSSEN

SAURON REDUX

The return of Sauron is signalled by his surprise attack on Minas Ithil in 3429 SA: the tower is taken, the White Tree is burned (Sauron may have hoped it was a case of second time lucky), and Isildur and his family are forced to flee up the Anduin and on to Arnor. For the Dúnedain, this is a shocking turn of events, since they believed Sauron had been destroyed in the Downfall. We might thus construe the network of fortresses built across western Middle-earth as being more about imposing power over local "Middle Men" populations (just as the Normans used motte-and-bailey castles to impose their regime on the Anglo-Saxons in post-Conquest England) than preparing for yet another struggle against the Dark Lord.

Given the history of the First and Second Ages – of which Elendil, Isildur and Anárion would have been fully aware – we may be also apt to think the Dúnedain to have been neglectfully complaisant. The attack on Minas Ithil, however, does provoke them into a greater state of war-readiness – Anárion retakes Minas Ithil the following year – and both kingdoms, in alliance with the Elves and other free peoples of Middle-earth, begin to prepare a counterattack against the resurgent Sauron.

MOUNT DOOM REAWAKENS
PETER PRICE

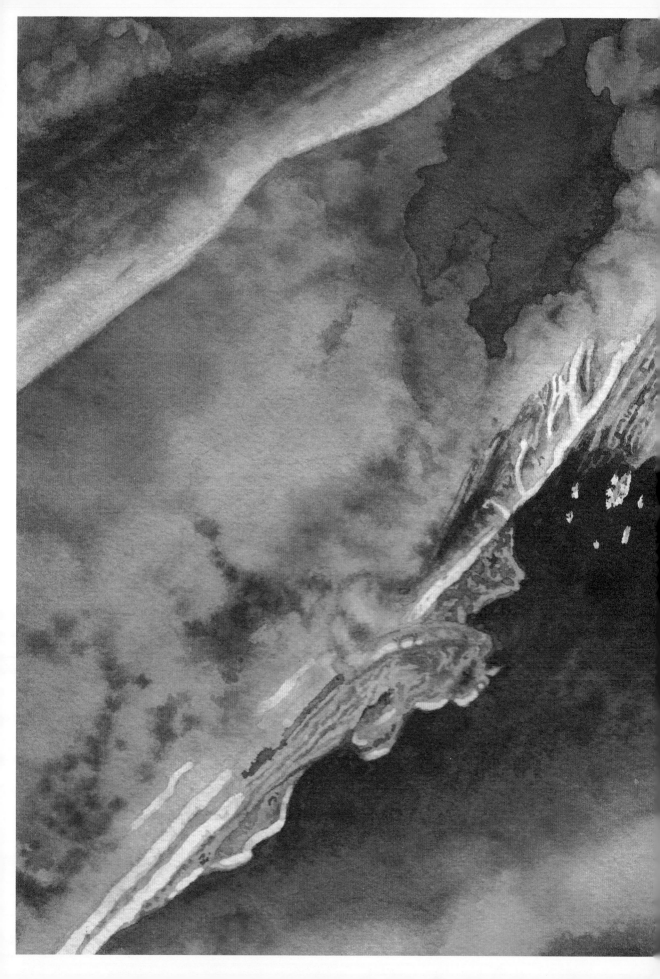

SOLDIERS ON THE HILL
IAN MILLER

THE WAR OF THE LAST ALLIANCE

Tolkien was certainly no stranger to war, nor to its tragedies. He served as an officer in the First World War, coming face to face with the abject horror of the trenches and losing two of his closest friends in the Battle of the Somme in 1916. In the Second World War, now too old to serve directly, he got to know war from the perspective of the home front, worrying about the two of his sons who were serving soldiers, while also facing the fears and privations of wartime, Blitz-hit Britain.

Many critics have seen Tolkien's writings as a response to the trauma of the First World War, even going so far as to see *The Lord of the Rings* as a "war novel", rather than as pure high fantasy. Tolkien himself admitted there were connections with the First World War, but denied vehemently there were any to the Second: Sauron is not Hitler; the One Ring is not the atomic bomb. There is a middle ground: *The Silmarillion* and *The Lord of the Rings*, along with many other of his writings, was to large degree a therapeutic process in which he faced up to and attempted to purge the trauma inflicted on him and his peers at the Somme, just as his story of the Downfall of Númenor helped him deal with his "Atlantis-haunting". His "mythology for England" was intended to be redemptive. We are not spared the horrors of war in *The Silmarillion* and *The Lord of the Rings*, but we, like the characters, are ultimately saved and redeemed, even if it takes a near-miraculous chain of events to achieve this "eucatastrophe", as Tolkien called it.

Who knows, then, what Tolkien might have made of the War of the Last Alliance had he written its tale in full? There are hints of the grandeur and terror it might have achieved: the Somme-like Battle of Dagorlad with the ill-considered charge of the Galadhrim and the swamp of bodies left behind in the Dead Marshes; the gruelling seven-year siege and the climactic, gruesome duel on the slopes of Mount Doom. What we do have, however, is an intriguing, almost medieval-style chronicle of its main events and manoeuvres – more than enough, then, to feed our imaginations.

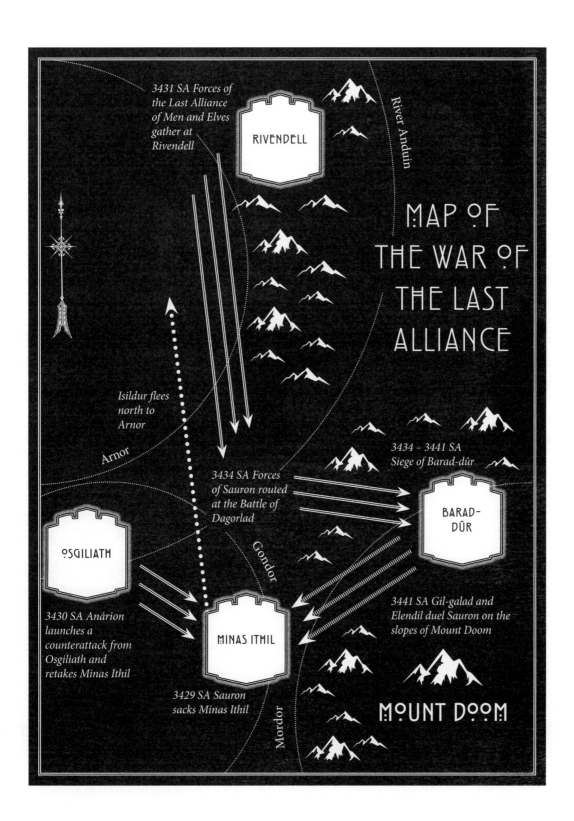

MAP OF
THE WAR OF
THE LAST
ALLIANCE

RIVENDELL

River Anduin

3431 SA Forces of the Last Alliance of Men and Elves gather at Rivendell

Isildur flees north to Arnor

Arnor

3434 SA Forces of Sauron routed at the Battle of Dagorlad

3434 – 3441 SA Siege of Barad-dûr

BARAD-DÛR

Gondor

OSGILIATH

3441 SA Gil-galad and Elendil duel Sauron on the slopes of Mount Doom

3430 SA Anárion launches a counterattack from Osgiliath and retakes Minas Ithil

MINAS ITHIL

3429 SA Sauron sacks Minas Ithil

Mordor

MOUNT DOOM

THE MOUNTAINS
ROBERT ZIGO

THE OATHBREAKERS

Throughout *The Lord of the Rings*, Tolkien skilfully weaves older histories into the present – the close of the Third Age, as portrayed in his epic novel, engages with and most often resolves many of the issues and problems raised in the Second.

One of these unresolved issues is that of the Oathbreakers – otherwise known as the Dead Men of Dunharrow. For much of the Second Age, the Men of the White Mountains are Men of Darkness but with the establishment of Gondor seem at least to recognize the Númenóreans as their lords, at last pay them lip-service. With the outbreak of the war against Sauron, the king of the Men of the White Mountains swears an oath of allegiance to Isildur at the Stone of Erech, but at the crucial moment fails to come to Gondor's aid. The bad faith of the Oathbreakers dooms them to an age-long wait as undead shadows in the hills, waiting for the prophesied time when they can finally make good their oath.

Tolkien's tale here is influenced by the central, sacred role oaths played in Norse society. Breaking an oath was an act of impiety which resulted in an individual's or group's expulsion from society. There was even a goddess Vár whose witness was called upon when oaths were made and who punished those who failed to keep them. Oathbreakers were condemned to Helheim, the world of the dead, just as the Men of the Mountain are.

Tolkien's Christian viewpoint allows for the ultimate redemption of the Oathbreakers. Aragorn's summoning of the Oathbreakers at the Stone of Erech during the War of the Ring allows them to finally fulfil their oath and to be released from the hell-like state in which they have been imprisoned.

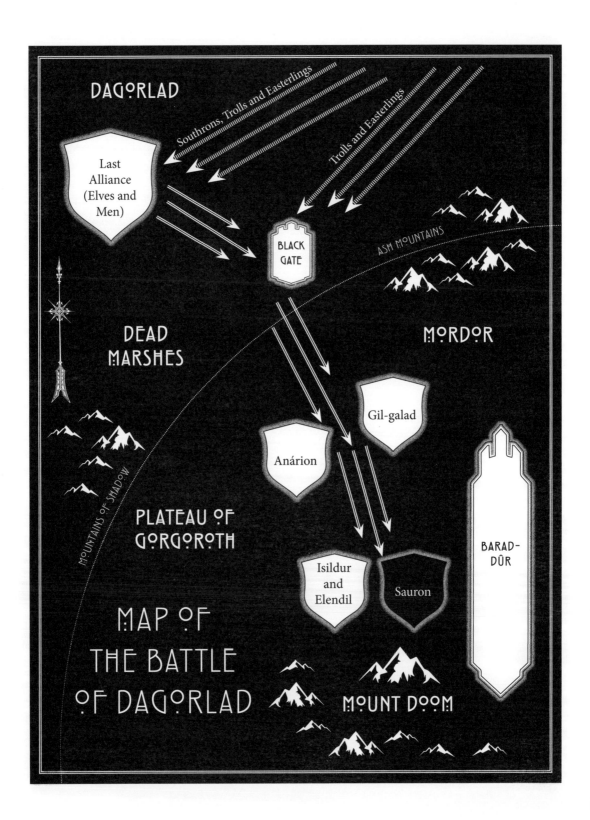

MAP OF
THE BATTLE
OF DAGORLAD

THE BATTLE OF DAGORLAD

One of the most memorable scenes in *The Lord of the Rings* is the crossing of the Dead Marshes by Frodo, Sam and Gollum. The travellers see spectral faces rising up beneath the greasy surface of the foul, brackish water. At this point the history of the Second Age quite literally surfaces in the Third: the faces belong to fallen Silvan Elves of the Woodland Realm and Lothlorien, slain in vast numbers during the Battle of Dagorlad – the first great battle in the War of the Great Alliance. We might imagine them to be the actual bodies of the buried Elves – preserved like the sacrificed, 2,000-year-old "bog bodies" discovered in peat bogs in the Irish Midlands – although Gollum claims they are only visions or spectres of the dead.

The power of the scene owes much to Tolkien's own experience as a soldier in the Lancashire Fusiliers during the First World War: once we know this, it is impossible to read the chapter "The Passage of the Marshes" in *The Two Towers* except through the lens of trench warfare – of the muddy, corpse-strewn battlefields of Verdun, the Somme and Passchendaele. Tolkien enlisted as a second lieutenant in the latter half of 1915 and after several months' training finally went to the Front (or close to it) in June 1916, shortly before the Anglo-French offensive known as the Battle of the Somme (July to November 1916). The first day of the offensive (1 July) remains one of the most notorious events in British military history – of the more than 120,000 British and French soldiers who took part in the assault, some 20,000 were killed, with many thousands more wounded or maimed. The territorial gains, by contrast, were painfully meagre. As a signals officer, Tolkien often worked behind the lines, but saw the brutal nature of war from close to, nonetheless.

The opening day of the Somme offensive seems to be recalled in the reckless opening assault carried out by the Galadhrim (Silvan Elves) under the command of Oropher of the Woodland Realm and King Amdír of Lórien, who chaffing under the overall leadership of High King Gil-galad and the Noldorin and Sindarin Elves, charged without waiting for orders and were decimated by Sauron's forces. The Galadhrim troops – Oropher and Amdír among them – were hastily buried in what, centuries later, would become the Dead Marshes.

Ultimately, most military historians argue that the Battle of the Somme did play an important strategic role in the development of the Great War – part of a process that saw the Allies take the tactical advantage away from the Germans and eventually claim victory in 1918 – though at an extraordinarily heavy cost, especially to the British who accounted for the vast majority of the casualties. The Battle of Dagorlad, costly in lives as it was, ultimately proved a victory for the Alliance, allowing Gil-galad to press on through the Black Gate towards the valley of Udûn and Sauron's fortress of Barad-dûr.

THE BATTLE
ALAN CURLESS

EARLY ORCS
TURNER MOHAN

SOMETHING WICKED THIS WAY COMES

One of our guilty pleasures as readers of *The Lord of the Rings* is revelling in the abundance of beasts and monsters – even if we see them only through the eyes of terrified Hobbits. Saruman's Uruk-hai, the "super-Orcs" bred in the pits of Isengard, or the more run-of-the-mill kind Frodo and Sam encounter in Cirith Ungol, both provide, in their rude language and ruder manners, a contrast to the heroic high-mindedness that is the rule among their opponents. In the Battle of Pelennor Fields before the gates of Minas Tirith, Tolkien offers up a smorgasbord of monstrous beings – Orcs, Orcs and more Orcs, trolls, bigger trolls, oliphaunts and the winged fell beast ridden by the Witch-king … Even if we are, of course, rooting for the good to win (which we know, of course, they will), we enjoy the downright hideousness and skulduggery that the evil brings to the narrative.

But where we may wonder are Sauron's fell allies in the Second Age? We know that his army was largely made of Men of Darkness – of Southrons, Easterlings and Black Númenóreans – but disappointingly there are no Ringwraiths, no Balrogs, no Dragons, no Wargs, no monsters at all except for the Orcs – at least none are mentioned. Tolkien's accounts of the battles of the Second Age, we have to remember, are epitomes – chronicle-like summaries – and so his focus is firmly on the main Elvish and Númenórean actors and events, not the down-and-dirty nitty-gritty of the battlefield. And yet Sauron must have undoubtedly made use of some or all of these foes – why would he not use every tool at his disposal? Perhaps it's down to us, when imagining the events of the Second Age, to deploy them out in the field.

THE GREAT BATTLE
IAN MILLER

BARAD-DÛR
DAVID ROBERTS

THE SIEGE OF BARAD-DÛR

The siege of a city or fortress has been an important element in warfare since ancient times. Most cities were built with powerful walls and other fortifications, so that they could not be taken with a rapid assault but had to be subjected to a long, costly campaign of attrition. Typical stratagems of siege warfare included the slow starving of the inhabitants by blocking (or sullying) supplies of food and water, the use of siege engines, bombardments and mining, and perhaps more underhand methods such as the recruitment of inside spies and traitors. The besieged population could fight back with their own weapons, such as missiles and Greek fire, but their real hope was that the besiegers would give up or they would be saved by the arrival of an ally, who could force an end to the siege. It is this latter indeed that brings a conclusion to the Siege of Minas Tirith in *The Lord of the Rings* – Tolkien's most sustained narrative account of a siege – where the plight of the city is ended by the arrival of the Riders of Rohan.

The most famous mythological siege is, of course, the ten-year siege of Troy, as told in part in Homer's *Iliad*, but in his brief account of the Siege of Barad-dûr, Tolkien may have also been thinking of any number of sieges from ancient and medieval history – for example the siege of Drepana (249–41 BCE), in which the ancient Romans besieged the Carthaginian naval stronghold for eight years. The Siege of Barad-dûr lasts almost as long – seven years, rather than eight – and is ended when Sauron leaves his fortress and challenges the leaders of the Alliance to single combat.

Siege warfare was often costly in lives for both the besiegers and besieged – not only was there the ever-present danger of weaponry but also epidemic disease such as plague. The only casualty Tolkien mentions during the actual siege is Anárion, who dies when he is struck by a rock or missile projected from the fortifications.

THE DEATH OF ANÁRION
MAURO MAZZARA

THE CHANSON DE GESTE

The epic character of certain chapters of *The Lord of the Rings* – especially in its latter half where the War of the Ring gathers pace and the book opens up to be more about the movements of whole armies, rather than the more small-scale, intimate journey of a small party of people (the "pilgrims' progress" of Frodo and Sam being one exception), has long been commented on. Not only the subject matter but the narrative tone, too, shifts quite dramatically, becoming grander, more archaic, even, some would say, more verbose. Not that the individual gets forgotten – there are still many more intimate moments – but they are now always set against a much wider historical tableau, small-scale actions entwined with the fate of nations.

One of the key influences on Tolkien in this respect is the *chanson de geste* – the French medieval epic in which heroes likewise act against a magnificent backdrop of battles and sieges but who are still occasionally witnessed at their more vulnerable, intimate moments. Such a moment occurs, for example, in the most famous *chanson de geste* – and the most influential on Tolkien – *The Song of Roland*, composed in the eleventh century. When Roland is ambushed by Saracens at the Pass of Roncesvalles, he only blows his oliphant horn when all is irretrievably lost and his only hope is to be avenged. It is at this moment that the narrative contracts to focus just on Roland and his dying breaths as he offers up his sword to God, his ultimate liege-lord. The scene was clearly a direct inspiration for the death of Boromir, and other similar moments abound in the account of the Battle of Pelennor Fields and elsewhere.

We also catch a glimpse of the epic but intimate atmosphere of *The Song of Roland* in Tolkien's admittedly epitomized accounts of the War of the Last Alliance, especially in the culminating duels between Gil-galad and Elendil, on the one hand, and Sauron on the other. In *The Lord of the Rings*, Sam begins to recite the opening verses of a *chanson de geste*–style poem entitled "The Fall of Gil-galad":

> Gil-galad was an elven-king.
> Of him the harpers sadly sing …

Tolkien may have intended to compose the entirety of "The Fall of Gil-galad", much as, beginning in 1925, he wrote a substantial fragment of the "Lay of Leithian", which he explicitly called a *gest[e]*: "The GEST of BEREN son of BARAHIR and Lúthien the FAY called TINUVIEL the NIGHTINGALE". Such a lay would surely have deepened our appreciation of Tolkien's achievement in laying out the historical sweep of the Second Age.

ROLAND / GIL-GALAD
MAURO MAZZARA

ELENDIL AND GIL-GALAD BATTLE SAURON
KIP RASMUSSEN

ARTHURIAN EPIC

Another "atmosphere" that overlays Tolkien's synoptic account of the War of the Last Alliance is the Arthurian epic (rather than the Arthurian romance), and most especially Sir Thomas Malory's *Le Morte d'Arthur* (1485), the Middle English prose compendium of Arthurian tales that culminates in the catastrophic Battle of Camlann between King Arthur and his son Mordred.

All of Tolkien's main characters in the War of the Last Alliance – Gil-galad, Elendil, Isildur, Sauron – have an Arthurian quality and behave almost like chivalric knights. Gil-galad – whose name may remind us of the perfect knight, Galahad – is, in his shining armour, the most Arthur-like figure, while Sauron, who is a kind of magnified Mordred – a figure whose death-like name may remind us of Mordor. Like the War of the Last Alliance, the Battle of Camlann ends in a duel, in which the participants die or at least appear to do so.

Sauron's behaviour in offering the duel is only explicable in heroic terms: what, we wonder, does he hope to gain by this move? While he has felt no such compunctions before, he now acts not so much like an invincible Dark Lord but as a Homeric, Arthurian or Norse (anti)hero who feels obliged to follow a code of honour.

SAURON DISFIGURED
MAURO MAZZARA

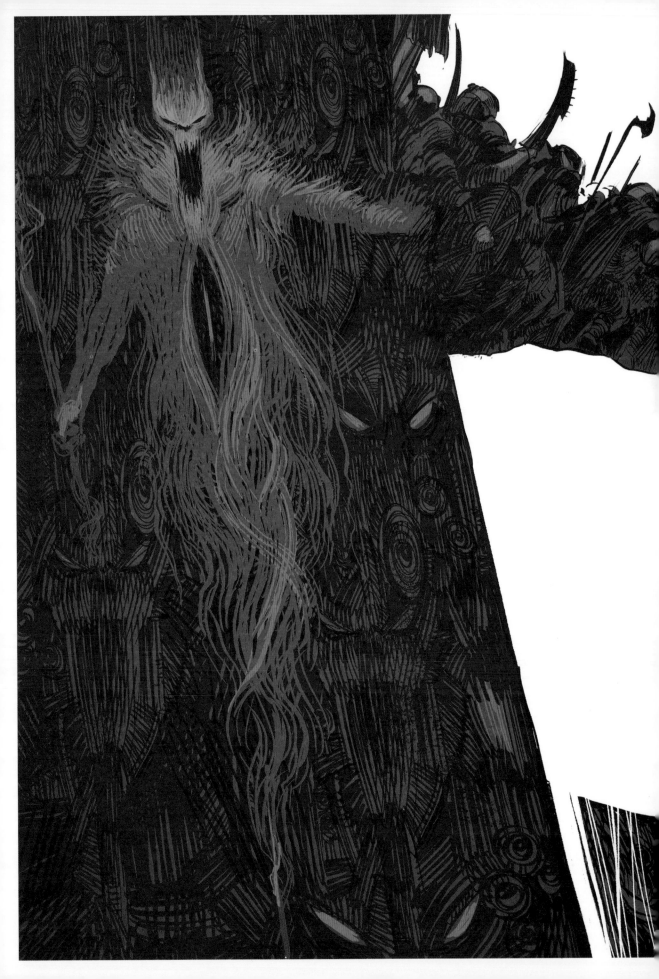

ELENDIL AND THE ONE RING
JOHN DAVIS

DUELS TO THE DEATH

The double duel between Elendil and Gil-galad – representing Númenóreans and Elves – and Sauron is the culmination of the War of the Last Alliance and, indeed, of the Second Age. It brings together in a single episode all the strands of its history – the fate of the Elves, the Downfall of Númenor and the forging of the Rings of Power. What might at first have seemed an age of rather disparate elements is here crystallized in a final, concentrated conflict: in this moment the grandeur of Tolkien's conception of the Second Age – perhaps unmatched by his histories of either the First and Third Ages – comes into sharp focus.

The duel to determine the outcome of a war is a feature of many mythological or legendary tales. In *The Iliad* we find, for example, a single combat duel between Paris and Menelaus, which ends abruptly when Aphrodite catches up her favourite, Paris, in a cloud to save him, as well as between Hector and Achilles, which ends with the Greek hero's victory and his gruesome treatment of his opponent's corpse.

Likewise in Norse mythology – reflecting a culture in which the duel, known as *hólmganga*, was used legally to resolve disputes – we find a plethora of Norse myths featuring trial by combat. The story of Ragnarök, the great final apocalyptic battle predicted to take place between gods and giants, is essentially a succession of duels: between Odin and the wolf Fenrir, Thor and the Midgard Serpent Jörmungandr, and so on. And, as we have seen, the great final battle in Sir Thomas Malory's *Le Morte d'Arthur* ends in a duel between the two leaders, Arthur and his son Mordred, in which both are mortally wounded:

> Then the king gat his spear in both his hands, and ran toward Sir Mordred, crying: Traitor, now is thy death-day come. And when Sir Mordred heard Sir Arthur, he ran until him with his sword drawn in his hand. And there King Arthur smote Sir Mordred under the shield, with a foin of his spear, throughout the body, more than a fathom. And when Sir Mordred felt that he had his death wound he thrust himself with the might that he had up to the bur of King Arthur's spear. And right so he smote his father Arthur, with his sword holden in both his hands, on the side of the head, that the sword pierced the helmet and the brain-pan, and therewithal Sir Mordred fell stark dead to the earth; and the noble Arthur fell in a swoon to the earth …

Tolkien's final three-way duel on the slopes of Mount Doom, described in summary, cannot have the drama of Malory's, but we can begin to see what he might have made of it in a Lay of Gil-galad: Gil-galad slain first by the heat of Sauron's hand; Elendil's fall and the breaking of his sword Narsil beneath his body; Sauron's own bodily destruction, and Isildur's use of Narsil's handle shard to strike off Sauron's ring finger. The fatal One Ring is at the beginning of its new long journey.

SAURON
JAROSLAV BRADAC

SAURON'S BODY

Sauron only appears to "die" at the Siege of Barad-dûr – his physical body may have been destroyed but his spirit is able to flee. In a ghastly way, his fate mirrors that of King Arthur, who after the Battle of Camlann is borne away to Avalon to be healed. Sauron too removes himself from the physical trappings of the world in order to heal and gather his force again, so that eventually, like Arthur, he can fight another day.

In his legendarium, Tolkien evolved a soul–body dualism that was of course heavily indebted to Christian and Platonic beliefs. On the one hand, there is the *fëa* – the enduring spirit of Elves, Men and other living, incarnate beings that come from Ilúvatar – and, on the other, the *hröa* – the house in which the fëa temporarily dwells during an individual's lifetime. With death, the fëa becomes houseless. Sauron, as a Maia, does not strictly follow this pattern – he can exist as pure spirit, which Tolkien calls *ëalar*, and only clothes himself in physical form. Nonetheless, from the perspective of incarnate beings, Sauron appears to suffer death during his duel with Gil-galad and Elendil and is later resurrected – just as, in *The Lord of the Rings*, Gandalf appears do die after his duel with the Balrog in Moria and is resurrected as Gandalf the White, or, indeed, Jesus appears to die at the Crucifixion and at Calvary is resurrected three days later.

DUAL SPIRITS
MAURO MAZZARA

THE FATE OF THE RING

Every good story ends with a new one, just as the end of the Second Age, coinciding with the defeat of Sauron, is also the beginning of the Third. When Isildur takes possession of the One Ring and, against all counsel, refuses to destroy it in the fires of Mount Doom, he initiates the story that will culminate in the events of *The Lord of the Rings*. His possession of the Ring and its possession of him set up a pattern that, almost three millennia later, will be echoed in the experiences of Gollum, Bilbo and Frodo. Only the last is able to fulfil what Isildur should have done. For Tolkien, stories, like history, are cyclical.

THE FATE OF THE RING
MAURO MAZZARA

THE ILLUSTRATORS

VICTOR AMBRUS

Victor Ambrus FRsa is a writer and illustrator and an Associate of the Royal College of Art, a Fellow of both the Royal Society of Arts and the Royal Society of Painters, Etchers and Engravers, and was also a patron of the Association of Archaeological Illustrators and Surveyors. He has illustrated many books for children and is now known from his appearances on the television archaeology series *Time Team*.

JAROSLAV BRADAC

Jaroslav Bradac studied at the Academy of Arts, Architecture and Design in Prague in the 1960s and moved to London in 1969. He works in a range of media and across many disciplines including sculpture and collage and has illustrated several books for adults and children. He animated and directed the animated version of "The Treatise" in the film of *Steppenwolf* (1974).

TIM CLAREY

Tim Clarey is an artist, painter and illustrator who has illustrated numerous children's books and covers for adult fiction. He studied illustration at Falmouth College of Arts and teaches illustration at Falmouth College.

ALLAN CURLESS

Allan Curless was a political cartoonist for 16 years, working mostly for the *Sunday Times*. His first children's book, *Cat's Song* with Andrew Matthews, was shortlisted for the Mother Goose Award and the Smarties Prize in 1994. He is perhaps best known for his chapter icon illustrations for Brian Jacques's *Redwall* series. He died in 1997.

JOHN DAVIS

Jon Davis is an illustrator, best known for his prolific career in comics including *Lady Penelope* and *TV Century 21*, and his illustrations for *Rupert the Bear* and Ladybird Books. He began his career in science fiction illustration after reading *The Hobbit* and *The Lord of the Rings*. He was awarded an MBE for services to Children's Literature in the Queen's New Year's Honours List in 2013 under his full name, John Frederick Charles Davis.

MELVYN GRANT

Melvyn "Mel" Grant is an artist and illustrator who, after a brief sojourn in Europe working as a guitarist and even designing and building some unusual electric guitars, returned to illustration work in various media, including animation. Grant has produced illustrations for many books, including the *Fighting Fantasy* gamebooks and is known for being one of the artists associated with Iron Maiden's mascot Eddie, and five of Iron Maiden's album covers.

LOST HILLS
PETER PRICE

BARBARA LOFTHOUSE

Barbara has worked as an illustrator since 1977. She has provided artwork for books, magazines, even for packaging. She prefers to work entirely in traditional media and as a result has found herself, over the past few years, doing less illustrations and moving into fine art.

PAULINE MARTIN

Pauline Martin studied at Brighton Polytechnic in the 1970s and developed an unusual and unique style of watercolour painting. She illustrated the beautiful *Moonlight and Fairyland* by Laurence Housman in 1978 and the following year contributed several exquisite pieces to *A Tolkien Bestiary*.

MAURO MAZZARA

Mauro Mazzara started drawing at the age of two and hasn't stopped. Published in the Annual Illustrators of Children's Books in 2002, Mauro joined the Brera Art Academy to study painting. He works as a freelance illustrator in publishing, fashion and advertising and teaches drawing and painting at Scuola Internazionale Comics in Brescia.

IAN MILLER

Ian Miller graduated from the Painting Faculty of St Martin's School of Art in 1970 and went on to become an artist, illustrator and writer. His film work includes two Ralph Bashki films, and pre-production on *Shrek* in the 1990s. The first collection of his work, *The Green Dog Trumpet* was published in 1979 by Dragon's Dream. This was followed shortly afterwards by a second volume entitled *Secret Art* and then *Ratspike*, co-authored with John Blanche.

ANDREW MOCKETT

Andrew Mockett is an artist and printmaker specialising in woodcuts and multiple screen-printings and has produced printed textiles for Givenchy and Paul Smith. He is currently represented by the Rebecca Hossack Gallery, in Conway Street, London and Mott Street, New York, and his work has featured in the public collections of several galleries including London's Tate Modern and Victoria and Albert Museum.

TURNER MOHAN

(James) Turner Mohan is a self-taught fantasy artist and illustrator based in Long Island, New York. His love of (and fascination with) history and mythology informs his fantasy illustration and he describes his incredibly detailed works as "a kind of fictional anthropology". He works in pen and ink but has also started to explore watercolour and sculpture and has recently been apprentice to a period-recreation armour maker.

ANDREA PIPARO

Andrea Piparo graduated from the Art School of via Ripetta and continued his studies by attending the illustration course at the International School of Comics. He has exhibited his works in various collective exhibitions and at various events such as Fantastika, Dozza (Bologna) in 2014 and at Wow Comics Space (Milan) in 2015.

PETER PRICE

Peter Xavier Price is a British artist, illustrator and academic historian. As an artist, he is known primarily for his illustrations of J.R.R. Tolkien's legendarium, particularly *The Silmarillion* and *The Lord of the Rings*. Alongside illustration, Price is an academic historian who studied at the University of Sussex, UK, from where he holds a doctorate in Intellectual History.

KIP RASMUSSEN

Kip Rasmussen is an illustrator, author and independent film producer. Inspired by the works of J.R.R. Tolkien, he interrupted his career as a family therapist to illustrate scenes from *The Silmarillion*, the work he considers more fundamental than both *The Hobbit* or *The Lord of the Rings*. His illustrations have been included in Peter Jackson's DVD "*The Hobbit*: The Desolation of Smaug". Kip is a published author as well as a producer of feature-length science-fiction and fantasy films.

DAVID ROBERTS

David Roberts began his career in fashion illustration before moving into children's book illustration. He has illustrated many books for children of all ages and is best known for his work with Julia Donaldson, Philip Ardagh and Chris Priestley. He has been nominated for the CILIP Kate Greenaway Medal, and in 2006 won the Nestlé Children's Book Prize Gold Award for his illustrations in *Mouse Noses on Toast*.

ŠÁRKA ŠKORPÍKOVÁ

Šárka Škorpíková is a Zoology student at Charles University in Prague but spends her free time painting and hopes to pursue a career in illustration and art stationery after finishing her course. She is a huge fan of Tolkien – *The Silmarillion* in particular – and draws on her love of wild landscapes when painting scenes from his works.

JAMIE WHYTE

Jamie Whyte is an artist and illustrator specialising in "creative cartography", which he defines as the creation of beautiful yet functional illustrated maps for print. As an illustrator and designer he has created artwork for fiction and non-fiction books, made logos for several companies and organisations and his work was recently featured in the three-part BBC4 history series *The Silk Road*.

ROBERT ZIGO

Róbert Zigo is a Slovak artist and photographer. His great passion is the world of fantasy and most of his illustrations are inspired by the works of J. R. R. Tolkien. Despite the fact that he studied law and worked as a lawyer, he decided to fulfill his dreams and devotes himself to art, graphics and photography and works as a professional photographer and freelance artist.